HELL HEAT

The lights in the old house flashed on and off wildly as the girl staggered down the stairs. She knew she had to escape the house, run for her life, get as far away as possible. She stumbled, almost falling headlong, then ran straight for the door. It was ajar and a strong gust of wind suddenly blew it open, slamming it against the wall. She screamed, thinking someone had thrown it open, then she turned.

With a powerful thrust, the sizzling, red-hot poker was driven straight into her stomach. It penetrated deeply, crisping her skin and sending thin tendrils of smoke curling up from the wound.

The breath hissed out of her as she felt the shock of the brutal impact and the fiery agony of the glowing iron. She saw the loathsome eyes behind the stark-white mask and then her vision blurred. . . .

FRIDAY THE 13th, PART 3

◯ SIGNET (0451)

FRIGHTENING FICTION

- ☐ **FRIDAY THE 13TH, PART I. Novel by Simon Hawke, based on the screenplay by Victor Miller.** Now a terrifying new TV series, this is the original and unequaled terror trip that started it all! (150899—$2.95)
- ☐ **SPHINX by Robin Cook.** Amid the awesome temples of Egypt's Valley of the Kings a fabulous treasure is waiting to be discovered, a treasure worth dying—or killing—for. The beautiful Erica Barow is threatened, overtaken and cursed by the ancient and modern worlds. "Passion and romance galore!"—*Playboy* (148711—$4.50)
- ☐ **SMALL WORLD by Tabitha King.** When Leyna Shaw awoke she was aware that something was different—terribly different. First she looked down at her tall, lovely body and saw no change. Then she looked around the room. It took her a moment to recognize it. It was the White House bedroom. And then she saw the Eye... and the Hand.... "Suspense so clever it could cut your skin."—Peter Straub. (136330—$3.95)
- ☐ **SLOB by Rex Miller.** A novel of shattering terror. "It really smokes, this writing!—Harlan Ellison. Jack Eichord, a Chicago homicide detective, trails a human monster and his hostages deep into the labyrinthian sewers. (150058—$3.95)
- ☐ **FRIDAY THE 13TH, PART III by Simon Hawke, based on the motion picture Friday the 13th Part III.** Chris was going back. Back to the place where she'd been found near-mad with terror. Back to prove that the horror was over once and for all. But was it really over? An un—invited guest was going along. His name was Jason and he was out to have a bloody ball.... (153111—$2.95)

Prices slightly higher in Canada

Buy them at your local bookstore or use this convenient coupon for ordering.

NEW AMERICAN LIBRARY
P.O. Box 999, Bergenfield, New Jersey 07621

Please send me the books I have checked above. I am enclosing $_____
(please add $1.00 to this order to cover postage and handling). Send check or money order—no cash or C.O.D.'s. Prices and numbers are subject to change without notice.

Name_____

Address_____

City _____ State _____ Zip Code _____

Allow 4-6 weeks for delivery.
This offer is subject to withdrawal without notice.

FRIDAY THE 13TH

PART 3

A Novel by
SIMON HAWKE

**Based on the motion picture FRIDAY
THE THIRTEENTH PART 3**

A SIGNET BOOK

NEW AMERICAN LIBRARY

PUBLISHER'S NOTE

This book is a work of fiction. Names, characters, places, and incidents either are the product of the author's imagination or are used fictitiously, and any resemblance to actual persons, living or dead, events, or locales is entirely coincidental.

NAL BOOKS ARE AVAILABLE AT QUANTITY DISCOUNTS WHEN USED TO PROMOTE PRODUCTS OR SERVICES. FOR INFORMATION PLEASE WRITE TO PREMIUM MARKETING DIVISION, NEW AMERICAN LIBRARY, 1633 BROADWAY, NEW YORK, NEW YORK 10019.

Copyright © 1988 Paramount Pictures Corporation. All Rights Reserved.

"FRIDAY THE THIRTEENTH PART 3" logo and artwork TM and copyright © 1982 Paramount Pictures. All Rights Reserved.

SIGNET TRADEMARK REG. U.S. PAT. OFF. AND FOREIGN COUNTRIES
REGISTERED TRADEMARK—MARCA REGISTRADA
HECHO EN CHICAGO, U.S.A.

SIGNET, SIGNET CLASSIC, MENTOR, ONYX, PLUME, MERIDIAN and NAL BOOKS are published by NAL PENGUIN INC., 1633 Broadway, New York, New York 10019

First Printing, May, 1988

1 2 3 4 5 6 7 8 9

PRINTED IN THE UNITED STATES OF AMERICA

For Phil and Pat,
who are far too hip for this sort of thing

PROLOGUE

Sometimes, Edna Hockett got so frustrated, she just wished she could die. Her life was going absolutely nowhere. She often wondered what the point of it was. There was no way out; she was stuck. And the worst thing was that she had done it to herself.

If anyone had told her back when she was seventeen that she would wind up married to a fat slob who ran a tiny roadside market way out in the middle of nowhere, just off a two-lane highway, and that her nights would be spent curled up on an old sofa in front of the TV, knitting sweaters endlessly just to have something to do with her hands so she wouldn't start pounding on the walls and screaming, she would never have believed it. But here she was, in her flannel nightgown and curlers in front of the TV in their living quarters over the store. They didn't even have a decent house to live in, not even a mobile home, just a lousy, cramped apartment above the store. How did she ever get herself into this mess?

When she had married Harold at eighteen, fresh out of high school, she felt so proud and free and full of life that it seemed as if nothing could hold her back. She married her high school sweetheart, the captain of the football team and the best-looking guy in school. Harold had a football scholarship to college and she planned on getting a part-time job to help make ends meet. They had wonderful plans. Harold was going to work hard and win a position as the starting quarterback in his sophomore or junior year. Then he'd get picked in the draft and spend some years playing pro ball, after which he'd take all the money he would have invested and start a business of his own. Well, Harold got drafted, all right, but it wasn't by any football team. This team was called the U.S. Army.

The big jerk just had to flunk out and get drafted. For a while, she was terrified that he'd get sent to Vietnam, but they shipped him off to West Germany instead, where he picked up a taste for dark beer and bratwurst and Wiener schnitzel and apple strudel. Pretty soon it was all that he could do to fit into his uniform. And after Harold got out of the army, he just kept on eating.

She couldn't really remember when she stopped calling him "honey" and started referring to him as "the big jerk." She wasn't sure when she started letting her own appearance slip, though she'd never allowed herself to get as sloppy and overweight as Harold. She couldn't remember when she'd finally realized that all her dreams were merely that—just dreams—and instead of "making it," she had started to settle for "just getting by." She was thirty-eight years old, but she looked forty-eight and sometimes she felt even older. She changed the TV channel with a sigh and sat back to see what bad news there was in the world.

The eleven o'clock news came on. "The quiet little community of Crystal Lake was shocked today with reports of a grisly mass murder scene," the anchorman said.

Her eyes grew wide and she leaned forward, staring intently at the screen. They were just down the road from Crystal Lake! She turned the volume up.

"Eight bodies have been discovered in what is already being called the most brutal and heinous crime in local history," the newscaster continued. "A police spokesman told 'Eye-On News' that they have been combing the area since just before dawn and are afraid that their gruesome discovery is just the beginning."

My God, she thought, it was almost like the last time, when that crazy Vorhees woman ran amok and killed those kids at that camp by the lake! Edna shuddered at the thought. "Camp Blood" was what all the newspapers had called it. And to think that Pamela Vorhees had actually been in their store every now and then! Who would have thought that a perfectly normal-looking woman like that . . . but these new murders couldn't have been done by her. She was dead. Edna remembered reading that she had been decapitated. She shuddered, imagining the gruesome sight of a body with its head cut off.

There was a crash outside and Edna jerked, startled by the noise. She ran over to the window and looked out. Of course, she thought, who else? It was Harold. The light of my life, she thought wryly. Some light. Some life.

He had stumbled into one of the poles holding up the clothesline and knocked it over. Now he was down there, flailing amid the hanging laundry, trying to get the pole propped back up. Looking at him now, at his clumsy, shambling gait, the awkward way he moved, his beer belly and fat cheeks and thinning hair, it was hard to believe that he had ever been a handsome young football hero.

It all just goes to show you, Edna thought. She had married the top jock, the best-looking boy in school, and look what he had turned into. On the other hand, her cousin Jennifer had married the class nerd and now he was a wealthy Hollywood screenwriter and Jennifer lived in a big house in Malibu, wore designer clothes and drove a fifty-thousand-dollar sports car. Go figure, Edna thought. Who would've guessed? Life was a cruel joke. She pushed open the window and leaned out.

"God*damn* it, Harold!" she screamed down at him as he looked up guiltily. "I spent all day yesterday washing your clothes and look what you're doing to 'em! You know I work very hard around here, tryin' to keep up with you and all your sloppy habits! And I get no help from you at all!"

She slammed the window back down furiously. "Jerk," she mumbled, going back over to the TV. They were still on the mass murder story. The anchorman had just turned it over to the reporter in the field.

"Police Chief Scott Fitzsimmons had no comment about the murders when reached early this morning," the reporter was saying as he stood outside one of the cabins down by Crystal Lake. In the background, an ambulance and police squad cars with flashing lights were visible. "Detectives at the scene, however, were baffled by the brutality of the killings," the reporter continued. "Bodies were found literally strewn over the four-square-mile campground in the remote lake region."

"Oh, my *God*," Edna murmured, biting her lower lip as she leaned forward slightly to adjust the antenna on the portable TV, improving the picture. She sat back again and resumed winding the yarn. The camera cut away to a shot of a pretty blond girl being taken out of the cabin on a stretcher. The reporter provided a voice-over commentary as she was loaded into the ambulance.

"Ginny Field miraculously survived repeated attacks by the ax-wielding killer and was taken to the hospital today," the reporter said, offscreen. "She is in serious condition, suffering from multiple stab wounds and severe hysterical shock. The names of the eight victims are still being withheld pending notification of next-of-kin. Reports of cannibalism and sexual mutilation are still unconfirmed at this hour. The person responsible for the Crystal Lake horror remains at large. . . ."

Edna reached forward quickly and turned off the TV. She didn't need to hear that sort of thing. My God, she thought, *cannibalism? Sexual mutilation?* And the killer was still at large? She wouldn't get a wink of sleep tonight.

"Harold?" she called, in a shrill voice. "What're you *doing* down there?"

There was no answer.

"Harold . . ." Edna set her mouth in a tight grimace. She hated it when he got sulky and didn't answer. "I *swear*. . . ."

She looked out the window, but there was no sign of him in the yard. Shaking her head, she put her knitting on the couch and went downstairs. She went out the back door into the yard, stood looking around for a moment, then glanced at the laundry hanging on the line and sighed. A work shirt and a pair of pants were missing. She picked up the basket and started taking down the clothes.

"Jesus Christ, Harold," she said, talking to herself, "you take what's yours and you leave the rest for me to do. So inconsiderate. Why didn't you just finish the job?"

No, of course not, that would be too much to ask, she thought. If I hadn't come out here to see what that big dope was doing, the laundry would've hung out here all night.

"Do I have to do *everything* around here?" she said to herself. Given the lack of response from Harold, she was saying things to herself more and more often. Christ, she thought, they'll be coming to take me away to the rubber room pretty soon. That's if I live so long.

She heard a footstep crunch on the gravel in the drive.

"Harold?"

She squinted into the darkness and, for a

moment, she thought she saw a large figure moving past, but now the sheets hanging on the clothesline blocked her view. She moved to look around them and saw that the door to the wooden shed out back was open. She put the basket back on the porch and went to see what the hell that jerk was doing out there in the middle of the night. Sometimes she simply couldn't figure him out at all. Most of the time, she thought, sourly.

Meanwhile, Harold was bent over the fishbowl in the back room of the market. He opened up a little can of fish food and shook some flakes out into the bowl.

"Okay, boys, soup's on," he said, shaking out far more flakes than necessary. In addition to overfeeding himself, Harold had a tendency to overfeed his pets. He had already fed the goldfish twice that day and now some instinct of self-preservation kept them from eating any more. "S'matter, aren't you hungry?" he said, coaxing them. "It's good. Here, look, I'm eating it."

He shook a few flakes out into the palm of his hand and licked them off. He smacked his lips, raised his eyebrows in appreciation, and shook some more flakes out into his palm. Not all that bad, he thought, giving the fish another taste. Wonder what's in 'em? He turned the can around to read the ingredients as he munched the flakes.

"Mayfly eggs?" he said, aghast.

He immediately began spitting out the flakes.

He heard a loud crunching sound and glanced up, wondering where it was coming from. Something was moving over in the produce section, by one of the vegetable bins.

"Hey, hey, hey, *hey!*" he shouted, dropping the fish food and running over to the produce section. He reached into the bin and pulled out a large white rabbit. "If Edna catches you in here, she's gonna make a fur coat out of 'ya!" he said, cradling the rabbit in his arms protectively. It looked up at him, snuffling its nose.

He sighed. What the hell, he thought, you can't blame the poor guy for being hungry. He grimaced wryly. Everyone was starving around here. If Edna had her way, he'd have the same diet as the rabbit—carrots and lettuce. What the hell kind of food was that for a man?

The thought of food made him hungry, and on his way toward the back door, Harold stopped and grabbed a jar of peanuts off one of the shelves. He looked around furtively, then twisted the lid open, breaking the vacuum seal. He shook out a handful of peanuts and popped them into his mouth, then carefully screwed the lid back onto the jar and replaced it on the shelf. Then he went over to the refrigerated section, took out a bottle of orange juice. After unscrewing the lid and washing down the peanuts with several swallows, he carefully replaced the lid and put the bottle back again. What the hell, he thought, nobody would notice. A man's gotta eat.

A box of chocolate-covered doughnuts caught his attention. He stared at it for a moment, his mouth watering. If he opened it, it wasn't like unscrewing a lid and only taking out a small amount that nobody would notice. Some customer would be sure to notice that the box had been opened and that there was a doughnut missing. On the other hand, they'd probably just figure that some kids had done it and they'd merely put the opened box back on the shelf and take a full one. It wasn't very likely that anyone would make a point of mentioning it to Edna. And if no one mentioned one missing doughnut, then they probably wouldn't mention two. No, thought Harold, they'd just put down the opened box and grab a full one and that would be the end of it. No one would complain and Edna would never know.

What the hell, he thought. He tucked the rabbit up in the crook of his arm and popped open the seal on the box. He licked his lips as he took out one of the moist, dark doughnuts and bit into it with gusto.

Behind him, the door opened soundlessly and a shadow crossed the floor.

Harold shoved the remainder of the chocolate doughnut into his mouth and greedily reached for another one. Holding it in his mouth, he closed the box back up and replaced it underneath several unopened ones. He'd remember where he put it so he could sneak some more later in the night if he wanted a late snack.

A shadow fell across him.

Harold turned, the doughnut still stuck between his teeth, and found himself face-to-face with Edna.

"Didn't I feed you enough for supper?" she shrilled at him, shaking her finger in his face. "The doctor said you have to lose weight, didn't he?" She sighed with exasperation. "You know, I *try* to help you, but you keep sneakin' food behind my back! What am I gonna *do* with you? And would you put that filthy animal back where it belongs? Come on!"

Harold looked down at the floor miserably as she went out, then he quickly grabbed another doughnut, crammed it into his mouth, and took the rabbit back out to the shed. He flicked on the light switch as he entered the shed, holding the rabbit in his arms and stroking it. But suddenly it started wriggling, panic-stricken, in his arms.

"Hey, hey, hey, what're you so nervous about?" said Harold, shifting his grip on the struggling rabbit.

He stopped for a moment as he approached the rabbit hutch and his mouth dropped open as he stared at the dead rabbits inside. He gasped and approached the hutch, shaking his head with disbelief.

"Who would *do* something like this?" he said, leaning close to the hutch and opening the door.

A huge copperhead rattlesnake reared up inside the hutch, its tail rattling a warning, its gaping mouth open, displaying the long, needle-sharp, curved fangs. Harold dropped the rabbit and recoiled just as it lunged at him, striking, its fangs missing his face by scant inches.

He ran panic-stricken out of the shed, holding on to his stomach with both hands. The sheer terror of his close call had loosened his bowels and he plunged through the back door, almost bowling Edna over as he made a beeline for the bathroom.

"What's the matter?" Edna shouted after him. "What happened?"

Harold mumbled something as he ran past her and bolted through the bathroom door, which he slammed behind him.

"It's all that crap you've been stuffing yourself with!" Edna shouted through the door. She shook her head in disgust and went back to the couch. She turned up the volume of the TV, then sat back down to her knitting. She scowled since one of the two long, steel knitting needles seemed to be missing. She looked all around on the couch and felt behind the cushions.

"Now where's that other needle?" she said, looking for it without success.

Harold sat on the toilet in the dilapidated bathroom, relieved that he had made it just in time. He never would have heard the end of it from Edna if he had gone in his pants. He had heard the expression "being scared shitless" before, but that was the first time he had ever experienced the literal truth of that saying. The only time he'd ever felt anything close to that kind of fear was when he was drafted and he didn't know if he would wind up going to Vietnam or not.

Thank God we'd already started pulling out by that time, Harold thought, reaching for the bottle of whiskey he kept hidden behind the toilet. He had been so terrified of being sent over there that he had started losing sleep and eating compulsively just to take his mind off it. Everyone had always thought that he was such a gridiron hero; they used to call him "Hockett the Rocket" because he scrambled in the backfield just like a pro, when the truth was that he scrambled so hard and so fast because he was absolutely terrified of being hit. The thought of being hurt completely unnerved him. And after all the horror stories he had heard about what went on in Vietnam, just the thought of being sent over there made his knees go weak. But he'd been lucky. Just like with that snake. Man, he thought, what a close call! He closed his eyes and sighed, then took another gulp of whiskey.

He had several of the bottles stashed away in the apartment and the store, as well as in the shed. They were all carefully hidden where Edna wasn't liable to find them. Fortunately, she wasn't much on cleaning lately, so most of the bottles went undiscovered. The place was a damn mess.

He uncapped the bottle and put it to his lips, taking several healthy slugs. It burned deliciously as it went down. God, how he'd needed that! The doctor had warned him about cutting back on the booze—well, what he'd actually said was, "If you don't stop drinking, Harold, you'll kill yourself"—but if having a rattlesnake almost bite your nose off wasn't enough excuse for a man to have a drink, he didn't know what was. Jesus, just being married to Edna was enough to drive a man to drink, he thought, knocking back another slug.

She was always on his back about his eating. Well, he thought, what the hell was there to do around here except eat? And drink a little on the sly. He hoisted the bottle once again. She was always complaining that he wasn't the man he used to be, that he wasn't the guy she'd married. He grimaced at the thought. Well, she wasn't exactly the girl *he'd* married, either. He remembered what she looked like back in high school. God, he thought, she was enough to make your heart stop. Long blond hair, incredible legs, and the way she had filled out her cheerleader's sweater, man, the guys used to fumble the ball every time she jumped up into the air, shaking her pompoms.

Now, she was always padding around the house in those ridiculous pink furry slippers, with her hair up in those pink plastic curlers and that flannel print housecoat covering what was still actually a pretty nice body come to think of it—only every time he tried to do anything she would groan and roll over on her side, saying, "God, not tonight, Harold, I'm really tired and I've got a headache."

Okay, so maybe he had put on some weight and maybe his hair had started falling out. Maybe he wasn't the same handsome, young quarterback she'd married, but hell, a guy couldn't help getting older, could he? She was always complaining that there was no more romance in their marriage. Romance! Try getting romantic with somebody whose head looks like a heating coil and whose face has about a pound of cold cream on it every night. Try getting romantic with someone who was always getting on your case about one thing or another, scolding you as if she was your mother, for cryin' out loud.

"Who can *live* like this?" she always said, spreading out her arms and looking up, as if expecting an answer from God.

"You tell me," he always replied. "This ain't no kind of life at all, if you ask me! Hell, the way things are goin', I might as well drop dead!"

"I sometimes wish you would!" she'd shout.

"And I wish I would, too!" he'd yell back, and then he'd stomp out of the room and go out to the shed, where he'd have a whiskey bottle stashed away.

He drained the whiskey bottle and wiped the liquor off his chin. I'm in the toilet, all right, he thought. For a moment, he felt like throwing the empty bottle against the wall, but then Edna wouldn't clean it up and he'd only wind up stepping on the broken glass the next time he came into the bathroom barefoot. He resisted the impulse and put the empty bottle down on the floor, reminding himself to get rid of it so that Edna wouldn't find it and give him a hard time.

He put the bottle behind the toilet, and as he straightened up, he noticed the dusty curtain opposite him move slightly.

The bathroom had two large cupboards in it, from which Harold had removed the shelves to make storage closets. One of the closets had a makeshift wooden door; the other was covered by a cloth curtain. The door had been missing for years and Harold kept meaning to replace it, but he never got around to it. Now he stared at the moving curtain, and it occurred to him that whoever had put the rattlesnake in with the rabbits might easily still be around. The closets were both deep enough for a prowler to hide in.

Harold swallowed nervously and pulled up his pants. He slowly moved over to the curtain and reached out to draw it aside. He hesitated. What if there *was* someone hiding in there? What would he do?

Hell, it's probably just my imagination, he told himself. That damn rattlesnake has got me spooked. He'd have to call someone tomorrow to get that damn snake out of the shed, because *he* sure as hell wasn't going back inside there. . . . On the other hand, maybe he'd send Edna in there.

Just to convince himself that he was getting worked up over nothing, Harold summoned up his nerve and jerked the curtain aside. There was nothing behind it except a pile of dusty cardboard cartons. He breathed a sigh of relief.

Then he glanced at the other closet.

He drew himself up and walked over to it, grasped the doorknob, turned it, flung open the door—and a large meat clever thudded into his chest with all the force of a lineman sacking a quarterback.

He staggered back, blood spurting from around the cleaver embedded deep in his chest, staring with horror and disbelief at the huge figure standing in the closet, and before the pain could even register, he died. He never felt the impact when his body fell upon the bathroom floor.

Edna heard the crash and scowled. "Harold?"

There was no answer. She reached out and turned off the TV.

"Harold?" she called again.

Why couldn't he ever answer when she called? It drove her crazy when he did that. With a sigh of exasperation, she got up and went over to the bathroom.

"Harold, you still in there?" she called through the door. "What was that crash? You break something again?"

No answer.

She tried the door. It was unlocked. She went inside and looked around. Now where the hell *was* he? She sniffed several times. Whiskey. It figured. She knew he hid his whiskey bottles all over the house, but she didn't even bother looking for them anymore. She was thankful that he wasn't one of those angry, nasty drunks. Whenever Harold had too much to drink, he would simply pass out, and at least then she'd get a little peace and quiet. Maybe one of these days he'd just pass out and never get back up, she thought. It would serve the big jerk right.

She heard a rustling sound behind the closet door. He was probably in there with his whiskey bottle. She jerked the door open and was confronted by a large rat sitting atop one of the storage cartons. She gasped and drew back from it with a grimace of disgust—and suddenly a large hand was clamped over her mouth and the missing steel knitting needle was driven through her neck, ripping through her voice box and emerging through her throat.

She struggled uselessly, realizing with horrifying clarity that she was being murdered. She gagged, choking on her own blood as it bubbled up into her throat, seeping between the fingers of the huge hand covering her mouth. Waves of white-hot pain washed over her, and then all sensation disappeared as numbness quickly spread throughout her body and she sank down into oblivion.

One

The group of small children playing baseball in the street scattered to make way for the silver, custom-striped van with the canoe and camping gear strapped to its roof. The teenagers inside grinned at the children who waited until the very last moment, asserting themselves with challenge in their eyes, before grudgingly getting out of the street. They could remember being much the same themselves not very long ago, regarding the street in front of their homes as turf rather than as a thoroughfare for cars.

"It's the white house on the left," said Chris, a shapely nineteen-year-old with reddish-brown hair, large eyes, and an energetic, slightly nervous manner. She pointed as they passed the house and pulled over to the curb on the opposite side of the street.

Andy and Debbie were both the same age as Chris. Andy was slim, with dark hair, brown eyes, an athletic build, and clean-cut, handsome looks. Debbie was slightly shorter than her boyfriend, with full, naturally wavy chestnut hair that fell down to her shoulders and a wide, sultry mouth. She had the kind of figure that would even attract attention in a sweat suit. They both stepped down out of the van and came around the back to join Chris as they crossed the street.

"Hey, Shelly," Chris called over her shoulder. "Come on out and meet your date!"

"Bring her to me!" a muffled voice called from the rear of the van.

Chris glanced back dubiously at Andy and Debbie, walking with their arms around each other. Andy merely shrugged. Debbie sighed and looked at him with a wry grimace. "Maybe this wasn't such a good idea," she said. She liked Vera and she regretted allowing Andy to talk her into setting up this blind date.

Andy grinned and kissed Debbie. Behind them, the rear door of the van opened and a chubby figure in faded jeans and a navy windbreaker came out, wearing a white mask and brandishing a huge knife.

Chris glanced at Andy and Debbie and shook her head. "Sex, sex, sex," she said. "You guys are getting boring, you know that?"

"So what would a weekend in the country be without a little sex?" said Andy, grinning.

"Cool it, Andy," Debbie said quickly, nudging him in the side and giving Chris an anxious glance.

Andy looked contrite. Debbie had told him what happened to Chris last summer, telling him to be careful of what he said around her, and he had already blown it. "I didn't mean it that way—" he said, apologetically. Chris interrupted him, not wanting to pursue it.

"I know you didn't," she said, reassuring him. The one thing she didn't need, especially this weekend, was to have her friends walking on eggshells around her because of what had happened to her. "Look, guys," she said, "I want you to have a good time this weekend. What happened to me at the lake happened a long time ago. I'm fine. Really. Forget about me."

Debbie looked concerned. She didn't fail to notice the way Chris had stiffened suddenly or the strained note in her voice as she tried to sound casual, as if it didn't matter. "I'm supposed to forget that we've been friends for—"

Andy yelled with surprise as the masked figure crept up behind him and plunged the knife into his back. The rubber blade bent as it struck his shoulder and Andy spun around angrily, grabbing the toy knife away and giving his "assailant" a hard shove.

"Damn it, Shelly!" he snapped. "Why do you always have to be such an asshole?"

"I beg your pardon," Shelly said stiffly from behind the mask, his tone arch and stagy, like a second-rate thespian's. "I'm not an asshole. I'm an actor." He broke the word up into two distinct syllables, so that it came out "ack-tor."

"Same thing," Andy said with disgust, angry with him for acting like a fool. Debbie and Chris walked away, shaking their heads. "Look, Shelly," Andy said, his tone softening, speaking to Shelly as if he were an awkward little brother, "you're my roommate and I like you . . . most of the time. But you gotta quit *doing* these things! Now, I set this date up for you, didn't I?"

Shelly remained silent, like a sullen child who was being scolded for misbehaving.

"Didn't I?" Andy persisted, leaning closer to him.

"Yeah . . ." Shelly said, morosely.

"So don't embarrass me," said Andy. "Just relax, be yourself!"

Shelly pushed the mask back up on his head. "Would you be yourself if you looked like this?" he said miserably.

There was actually nothing wrong with the way he looked, except that he was very overweight, which gave his body and his features a round and pudgy softness. His light brown hair was very curly, and while he wasn't ugly, by any means, his poor self-image gave him a sort of hangdog expression that telegraphed his own unhappiness with the way he looked to others. And when Shelly was unhappy, Shelly ate, and the more he ate, the heavier he became, and the heavier he got, the more his unhappiness increased. It was a vicious cycle. Frustration led him to seek gratification in food, which only made the problem worse and led to more frustration and size double-extra-large.

Disappointed with reality, Shelly found escape in fantasy. Movies were his drug. He saw several each week, often going to two or three in a row on weekends. At first, it had been enough merely to sit inside a darkened theater and watch another reality unfolding on the screen, but as he got older, he became more and more involved with his fantasy world that he preferred so much to his own.

He became a walking encyclopedia of movie trivia. He read up on the art of filmmaking and learned about camera techniques, special effects, and makeup. He became an expert on who was doing what in films, always staying at the end of every movie to see the credits and remember who had done the editing, the special effects, the stunt work, the music, and the costuming. He began to experiment with theatrical makeup and latex molding and soon everyone he knew became exposed to the many faces of Shelly Greenblatt. The drama club at school was not enough to give vent to his creative impulses; the whole world became his stage. The only problem was, he often did not know when to stop.

He and Andy had been roommates since they had started college, and although Andy knew Shelly well enough to understand him and make allowances for his behavior, it was often extremely frustrating trying to make excuses for the way he acted. He often wished Shelly wouldn't try so hard. He had hoped that taking Shelly with him on this weekend would help him to unwind a bit and drop the goofball act. He had even asked Debbie and Chris to fix Shelly up. Yet now it looked as if the whole thing might have been a bad idea. The pressure was apparently making Shelly very nervous, and when Shelly became nervous, he acted like a nerd. Andy hoped the weekend wouldn't turn into a disaster.

They walked up the front steps onto the porch of the white house and Chris rang the bell. Shelly hung back slightly, looking like an inmate about to walk his last mile on death row. The door was opened by a middle-aged Hispanic woman who spoke to them with a slight accent.

"Yes?" she said, eyeing them coolly.

"Hi, Mrs. Sanchez," Chris said, with a smile. "I'm Chris. We've come to pick up Vera."

"She's *not* going," Mrs. Sanchez snapped, and slammed the door in their faces.

They exchanged startled glances. They had absolutely no idea what had caused such a reaction. From inside the house, they heard Vera and her mother shouting at each other in rapid Spanish.

"What're they saying?" said Chris, glancing uncertainly at Debbie.

Debbie shrugged helplessly. "I don't know," she said. "I flunked Spanish."

They were about to leave when the door opened once again and a striking, raven-haired twenty-year-old in a form-fitting blouse and tight shorts came out onto the porch, carrying a knapsack over her shoulder. Shelly's eyes bulged.

Vera smiled awkwardly, slightly embarrassed at the scene she knew they must have overheard. "Hi, everybody," she said. "What're you looking at? Let's go."

"Is everything all right?" said Chris.

Vera shrugged. "You know, just your basic, old-fashioned mother problems. So, which one's my date?"

Shelly stepped out from behind Andy. "Hi," he said sheepishly, practically shuffling his feet.

"You're Shelly?" Vera said, unable to hide her disappointment.

He sighed apologetically. "Sorry."

That's what I get for agreeing to go out on a blind date, thought Vera. Her mother had been outraged at the idea: not only was Vera going out on a date with a boy she'd never even seen before, she was going away for the weekend! Vera's mother was very traditional and she thought that the whole thing was scandalous. She had forbidden her to go, which of course had been a sure way to guarantee that Vera went, no matter what. Now it was too late. If she backed out now, her mother would never let her hear the end of it. Like it or not, she was stuck with this guy for the whole weekend. The expression on her face clearly mirrored her thoughts.

Andy rolled his eyes. Debbie had been right. This wasn't such a great idea. Why had he insisted on bringing Shelly along? The weekend was going to be death.

"Hey!" Debbie shouted, pointing. *"The van's on fire!"*

Smoke was billowing out of the windows in the van. They ran across the street and threw open the doors, but instead of a fire, they were confronted with the sight of Chuck and Chili, sitting cross-legged on the floor in the back of the van with imbecilic grins on their faces, puffing away on plastic bongs that were so huge they looked like oboes. The sickly-sweet smell of marijuana smoke permeated the van's interior. In order to dissipate some of the smoke, Chris and Andy rolled the windows down all the way as they drove off. All they needed was to get pulled over for speeding or running a stop sign and have a cop take one whiff inside that van. It would be all over.

Shelly watched disapprovingly as Chuck and Chili organized their stash. Chuck was a round-faced nineteen-year-old with a full black beard and a headband holding down his bushy hair. He wore well-faded jeans and tinted aviator glasses. With his sixties look, Chuck might have stepped right out of a time warp. His girlfriend, Chili, was a darkly attractive, slim eighteen-year-old with curly black hair and a facial expression that made her look as if she was always pouting. Chili was actually her real name. She had a twin sister named Pepper. The girls were born in a commune in Santa Fe and their parents were a little loaded at the time.

"Is that all you're going to do this weekend?" said Shelly disapprovingly, watching them sort their plastic sandwich bags filled with grass. "Smoke dope?"

"Why not?" said Chuck wryly. "There's no law against it."

He seemed to find his comment extremely funny. But then, dopers were liable to laugh at anything, thought Shelly. He shook his head.

"There's better things to do with your life," he said.

"Like what?" said Chuck.

"I can't think of anything," said Chili.

Shelly decided to forget about it. It wasn't his business to tell other people how to live their lives, but he wished that people that insisted on their right to ruin their health would respect other people's rights as well. He wasn't crazy about having to sit there and breathe in their smoke. It was as bad as actually smoking.

"Hey, Chrissie," Andy said, "how much farther to the lake?"

"We could've been there already if some people didn't have to go to the bathroom every five minutes," Chris said wearily, glancing pointedly at Debbie.

"That's what happens when you're pregnant," Debbie said defensively. She had only known about it for a month or so and she hadn't started to show yet. She also hadn't told her parents. They didn't even know that she and Andy were sleeping with each other, much less planning to get married. They figured she was still going out on casual dates.

Chili offered a joint to Vera, who was sitting between Chuck and Shelly in the rear of the van. "Sure, why not?" said Vera, taking it.

Shelly couldn't take his eyes off her. Those shorts were so tight, they looked as if she had been poured into them and she was sitting with her legs spread . . . and her blouse was unbuttoned enough that if she leaned forward a little, or if he leaned back, he could see . . .

When Vera turned and caught him staring down her blouse, Shelly quickly looked away. Now she probably really thinks I'm a jerk, he thought, angry with himself. He could never seem to do anything right. Hell, he thought, can you blame a guy for staring when a girl's dressed like that? How can you *not* stare at anybody who's so incredibly gorgeous? And she was supposed to be his date, too! A blind date, but still, he'd never had a date with anyone who looked like her. And he probably never would again, he thought miserably.

"Hey, let's share the wealth with those less fortunate up front, huh?" said Andy.

Vera passed the joint to him and sat back down beside Shelly. Her gaze fell on the small black case where he kept his props and makeup. She looked up at him with curiosity. "What've you got in there?" she said.

"My whole world," he said mysteriously.

"In *that* little thing?" said Vera, amused.

"Stick around," said Shelly. "You'll see."

Vera shrugged and turned to look out the back window. She saw flashing red lights in the distance. They were coming up fast, and a second later she heard the sirens.

"It's the cops!" she said.

"What?" said Debbie.

Chris glanced into her sideview mirror. "Oh, *no!*" she cried.

"Oh, my *God!*" said Chili.

"What're we gonna *do?*" moaned Shelly, anxiously looking out the back window as the two police cars came up fast.

"Destroy the evidence!" said Vera, grabbing for the plastic bags.

Chuck snatched them back from her. "No way, man!"

"Let *go*, Chuck," Chili said. *"Come on!"*

It took a moment for it to sink in. Then he suddenly realized what would happen if they were pulled over with all that dope in their possession.

"We gotta get rid of it!" he cried, panicking as the sirens rapidly approached.

Andy grabbed a bag. "Eat it!" he said, stuffing some into his mouth.

They started stuffing the loose joints and the grass into their mouths, swallowing as quickly as they could. When Chuck realized that they were never going to get it all down in time, he tossed a bag to Vera, who started stuffing the grass into her mouth and swallowing as fast as she could.

"The cops are going to get us!" Shelly wailed. "We're going to jail!"

Andy held a bag out to Chris.

She shook her head. "I'm driving."

He turned to Debbie and held the bag out to her.

"No way!" she said emphatically. "We're pregnant, remember?"

The police cars were almost on top of them. Chris kept glancing nervously into the sideview mirror.

"Faster, faster!" Chili said, chewing furiously and swallowing as quickly as she could. "You better step on it!"

Chris sped up, but the police cruisers kept on gaining.

Their cheeks were all stuffed to capacity.

"Faster! Eat faster!" Shelly cried.

"Come on, *help* us!" Vera said, handing him a fistful of grass. "Come *on!*"

"Uh . . . I guess I'm just not hungry," Shelly said, grimacing with distaste and pulling back from her.

"You're *always* hungry, Shelly!" Andy said, his mouth full. "Come on, *eat!*"

"Come on, hurry *up!*" said Vera.

"I'm allergic to pot!" Shelly shouted, furious that he was going to get busted because of them.

"They're too close!" said Chris. "I gotta pull over!"

They all started cramming dope into their

mouths as the van pulled over onto the shoulder and stopped.

The two police cruisers shot right past them without even slowing down.

For a second, they all stared out through the windshield with disbelief, and then they sighed with relief. A few seconds later, it occurred to them that they had eaten almost all their stash.

"Oh, *man!*" moaned Chuck.

"Oh shit!" said Chili, trying to scrape together the grass they'd dropped onto the floor of the van.

Chris wondered where the police cars could possibly have been going that they had ignored them like that. She had been driving well over the speed limit, trying to buy the others some time to get rid of the dope. A few miles down the road, she had her answer.

To the left, there was a turnoff sloping downhill to a small roadside grocery store at the foot of the highway embankment. The police cruisers pulled in with screeching tires, and the officers jumped out of their cars and hurried over to the store.

"Okay, you guys, show's over," one of them said, beckoning the small group of people away from the store entrance. "Let's move it back over here, all right?"

There was an ambulance parked in front of the entrance to the market. Chris slowed down as the road followed the curve of the embankment so that they could look down as they passed and see what was going on. As they drove past the market, the ambulance attendants came out, carrying two stretchers with sheet-covered bodies strapped to them. Chris couldn't take her eyes off the sight. She swerved sharply and snapped out of it, quickly returning her attention to the road.

"Hey, kiddo," said Debbie gently, seeing the expression on her face, "don't let your imagination run away with you."

Chris swallowed hard, trying to calm down. Her nerves were already more than a bit on edge just at the thought of coming back to Crystal Lake again. And now this . . .

"Chris, stop the van!" cried Debbie.

"What?" she said, startled, snapping out of her reverie. "What is it?"

"Stop!"

Chris slammed on the brakes.

She was not a moment too soon. The van screeched to a stop inches away from an old man lying in the center of the road.

"What are you doin'?" Andy said. "You almost ran over him!"

"I . . . I must have been daydreaming," said Chris, shocked at what she almost did. "I didn't even *see* him!"

They piled out of the van and approached

the motionless figure. He was lying on his back in the middle of the road, his head pillowed on a duffle bag. It was a hell of a place to take a nap. He was in his late sixties or seventies, and had stringy gray hair and a long beard. He was as skinny as a rake, his old baggy clothes were badly in need of a washing and his face was covered by a beat-up straw hat. He didn't move a muscle.

"Hey, man, he looks just like my grandfather!" said Chuck, bending over him.

They stood around the old man, looking down at him with concern. As their shadows fell across him, his eyes fluttered open.

"Why," he said, looking at Debbie and Vera and speaking in a wheezy voice, "I must be in heaven!"

Chuck grinned. "What're you doin' down there, old guy?" he said.

"You all right?" Chris asked him in a worried tone.

"Get him up," said Andy.

"Don't touch him!" Shelly cautioned, keeping well back from the old man. "You don't know where he's been!"

"Thank you, thank you, thank you," the old man said as they helped him to his feet. "You are, indeed, all of you, kind and generous young people. Look upon what His Grace has brought me!"

He reached into his pocket and withdrew a curious-looking, slimy, whitish object. His hand trembled as he held it out, directly under Shelly's face.

Shelly winced, looking down at the disgusting looking object and wrinkling his nose. "What *is* that?" he said.

"I found this today," the old man said, gravely. "There were other pieces of the body...."

"That's an eyeball!" Shelly cried, gasping and recoiling from the object.

"He wanted me to have this," the old man said, showing them the eyeball and glaring at them wildly. "He wanted me to warn you!"

They rushed back toward the van and piled in as the old man staggered after them, brandishing the eyeball, his voice rising in pitch like an evangelical preacher's.

"Look upon this omen!" he cried as Chris quickly started up the van and shifted into gear, pulling around him in a wide circle. "And go back from whence ye came!"

Chris floored it and the van shot down the road, leaving the old man in its dust.

"I have warned thee!" the old man shouted after them, waving the eyeball at the rapidly receding van. "I have warned thee!"

TWO

The letters carved into the heavily weathered, swinging wooden sign mounted on a post by the packed earth driveway read HIGGINS HAVEN. The old lakeside vacation home was set in a grove of large oak trees that had been there long before the house was built. Their heavy branches hung low over the driveway. The weather-beaten frame house had an elevated porch and curtained windows. Unlike many of the homes in the area, it wasn't a Victorian or New England style, but sort of a bastardized amalgamation of the two.

In front of the porch, there was a large, packed earth parking area where the drive curved around and ran over to the ancient barn, some thirty yards to the left and slightly to the rear of the house. There were bales of hay piled up in a penned-in area near the front of the barn, and the window doors to the hayloft were open, displaying an old block and tackle for hoisting up the bales.

About twenty-five yards to the right of the house was an old outhouse with a peaked roof and a traditional half-moon vent hole in the wooden door—a relic of time before the house had been equipped with modern plumbing. Past the outhouse and down a slight incline was the lakeshore where an old wooden boat dock jutted out some twenty feet over the water.

Chris turned into the entrance and drove over an ancient, loose-planked wooden bridge that spanned a dried-up streambed that curved around the house.

"Check it out!" yelled Andy as they turned into the driveway and approached the house.

Chris pulled the van up in front of the porch and stopped. They all jumped out and ran immediately down to the lake.

"Why don't we take our bags into the house first?" Chris shouted after them, but like restless kids needing to release pent-up energy after a long car trip, they paid no attention to her. She shrugged and sighed.

"Chris! Come on down!" shouted Debbie from the dock.

Chris shook her head. "You go ahead," she called to her. "I'm going to take my bags in the house first and look around."

Behind her, inside the house, someone parted the curtains slightly and looked out.

Chris turned back toward the house and the figure in the window disappeared. For a moment, she stood still, simply staring at the old place. It seemed like a long time. A very long time. Almost as if it had been another life. Then she took a deep breath, grabbed her duffel bag, and climbed the porch steps to the front door.

Her parents hadn't wanted her to come here, nor did they want to come here anymore themselves. They kept talking about putting the old place on the market, but somehow they never got around to it, as if they simply didn't want to deal with anything that touched it. As if what had happened to her was *their* problem.

Well, it *wasn't* their problem, she thought bitterly. It was hers. What had happened had happened to her, not to them. They didn't seem to understand that. She was the one who had to deal with it, one way or another. Avoiding it was not the answer. Your problems didn't disappear if you ignored them. The only way that she could think of facing what had happened to her was to come back here and deal with it once and for all. Come back to Crystal Lake where the nightmare had begun.

She started to look for the keys to the front door and then noticed with surprise that the door was slightly ajar. She frowned. There wasn't supposed to be anybody here.

"Hello?" she said uncertainly.

There was no response. Glancing over her shoulder toward the lake where her friends were, she hesitantly took hold of the doorknob and pushed open the door. It opened with a creak and she stepped inside.

With all the curtains drawn, the house was dark. Only faint gleams of sunlight penetrated through the gaps in the faded window curtains, sending thin shafts of light across the floor.

"Is someone here?" she said nervously.

Suddenly she felt a hand grab her by the neck and yank her backward sharply. She gasped, opening her mouth to scream, but before she could, she was pinned against the wall and felt herself being kissed passionately. Opening her eyes wide, she broke the kiss, pulling back, and gave her "attacker" a hard shove.

"Rick!" she said, enormously relieved and yet at the same time really angry at being scared like that. She hadn't expected to run into him here, at least not this soon, but then she realized that he must have been working out in the barn, hauling in the hay, when they had driven up. Her father had obviously forgotten about stopping the delivery and Rick

was just being helpful, trying to get it in before it rotted. He probably didn't know that her family wasn't coming this summer, that they were probably never coming back again. She had never told him about what happened, and as a result, there was no way he could have known what coming back here again meant to her.

"Is it just my imagination or did it just get cold in here?" said Rick, sounding disappointed.

Rick was a tall, attractive, well-built twenty-three-year-old with short dark hair and an easy smile. He was dressed in a plaid work shirt and jeans and he leaned against the wall, watching Chris uncertainly, the puzzled expression on his face saying he didn't know what he had done wrong. She gave him an exasperated look and walked away from him, trying to collect herself.

"Did I do something wrong?" said Rick, coming toward her with a look of concern on his face.

She turned back to him with a sigh. "No . . . it's just being here again," she said, not sure how to make him understand. She really didn't want to get into it now. She wasn't ready for him. Not yet, it was too soon. "I know it's only been a year," she said, "but I feel like I've been away forever."

Her gaze went around the room. "It doesn't

look like anything's changed, though," she said, sighing wistfully. "Even the paintings are still crooked."

She went over to the wall and straightened one of the inexpensive landscape paintings. Her father had bought them at a "starving artists" warehouse sale, thinking he had found a real bargain, and later had found out that the "starving artists" were starving in Korea, where they were being paid slave wages to turn out hundreds of copies of the same landscape scenes for export.

"You've certainly changed," said Rick, watching her, unable to understand her standoffishness. "Don't you even say hello anymore?"

"I'm sorry," Chris said, turning back to him. She forced a smile. "Hello, Rick. How are you?"

He smiled uncertainly. "Well, that's a start."

He reached for her and bent down to kiss her once again, but she pulled back, retreating from him.

"Could you just *slow down* please?" she said. "There's a whole weekend ahead of us. Let me get to know you again. Let me get to know this place again."

"Okay," said Rick, with a grin. "But there's only just so many cold showers I can take."

Chris rolled her eyes. "Come outside and help me with the bags," she said.

Lighten up, Chris, she told herself. He doesn't

understand. How could he? A year ago this time, they had been discovering something really special together. They were starting to get serious and talking about the future in a way she hadn't thought she'd be ready to discuss for a long time yet, and then her whole world had caved in.

Rick didn't have a clue about what happened. At her family's request, it had been kept out of the papers and she had never told him, never bothered to explain, because she couldn't. She simply couldn't. She had not been able to deal with it herself, how could she expect him to accept what had happened to her? She was afraid to tell him.

So far as he knew, she and her family had simply gone back home. He wrote her letters asking what happened, and she wrote back, pretending that something had come up at the last minute—something to do with her father's business—and they had to leave at once; there had been no chance to say good-bye. They had kept in touch, but Rick was not much of a letter writer, and on the occasions when he called, she was either noncommittal or she pretended that she wasn't home. He wasn't stupid. He knew something was wrong, but he did not know what it was and he was trying to pick up where they had left off—to recapture what they had last summer. She really wished they could, but no longer knew if it was possible.

Still, it's not his fault, she told herself as they went outside. And she really was happy to see him. Maybe it would be easier with him around. Loosening up a little, she jumped, laughing, onto his back and threw her arms around him as he preceded her down the porch stairs.

"Ooof!" he grunted, exaggerating the strain as he carried her piggyback. "You know, Chris, I think you've gained some weight since last summer."

"I have not!" she said, punching him playfully. "You creep! Put me down!"

He dropped her at the van. "Here," he said, reaching up to untie the ropes holding down their gear and the canoe, "get the ones inside. I'll get the ones on top."

She went over to the side door of the van. It was partway open. She paused, looking at it uncertainly. "Wasn't this door closed just a few minutes ago?" she said to herself.

"What did you say?" said Rick as he grabbed the bags off the top of the van and started to carry them back up to the house.

Chris shook her head. "Nothing." She looked around, took a deep breath, and exhaled heavily. "Chris . . ." she said, admonishing herself.

She had only just arrived and already she was getting paranoid. This wasn't a good sign. First she gave Rick a hard time about greeting her with a kiss and almost giving her a heart attack, as if it were his fault about what happened, and now this. She was feeling jumpy about an open door, as if someone had crept into the van when nobody was looking and was waiting to leap out at her. She had to get things back under control. She couldn't go through life overreacting to every little thing. She reached into the van for a bag and jumped back with a small cry as a hand closed round her wrist.

"That's *my* bag," Shelly said protectively, sticking his head out of the van and taking his makeup case from her. "I'll take care of it."

"Shelly!" she said, not so much angry with him for startling her as angry with herself for being so jumpy. "What are you doing in there? Why aren't you down at the lake with everybody else?"

"Oh, they said they were going skinny-dipping," he said with a self-deprecating grimace, "and I'm not skinny enough."

He couldn't even bring himself to take his shirt off in public. Back in high school, the locker room during gym class had always been horribly traumatic for him. He hated it when guys came up to him and grabbed his flabby pecs, saying things like, "Hey, come on, honey, let me cop a feel," or "Hey, Shelly, what cup size do you take?" They thought it was extremely funny, but it hurt. It hurt incredibly and filled him with such overwhelming self-loathing that he promptly went out to a pizza joint and pigged out on a large deep-dish pie with the works and a pitcher of soda. There was no escape.

He watched Chris as she walked back to the house with Rick and sighed. It looked like everybody had somebody. Everybody except him. Debbie and Andy were coming back up from the lake, arm in arm, and Chuck and Chili were off somewhere getting stoned together. There was Vera, "his date," though she acted as if he didn't even exist. He wondered, longingly, what it would be like to have someone like Vera. Yeah, sure, he thought, fat chance. And fat was the word, all right.

Chris opened the door and stood aside for Debbie as she came in from the balcony corridor. "This was my bedroom," she said. "It's yours for the weekend."

"Great," said Debbie, looking around at the homey little room. She raised her eyebrows in puzzlement and turned around, her gaze sweeping the room. "Chris, I don't mean to be picky or anything, but where's the bed?"

Chris had gone to the window to pull aside the drape. The window looked down at the barn, and she noticed the barn door slowly swinging shut. She wondered who had gone inside there. Probably Rick, she thought, and turned back from the window.

"Chris?" said Debbie.

"Oh, it's right here," Chris said, turning around and opening a small, swinging partition to reveal a net hammock slung up on a hook.

"What's this?" said Debbie, looking at her to see if she was joking.

"It's your bed," said Chris, with a straight face.

"A *hammock?*"

"You might like it," Chris said with a grin, imagining her and Andy in it together as she went out the door.

Debbie shrugged gamely. "Why not?" she said, lifting off one end to stretch the hammock out to the opposite hook. It couldn't be any worse than the backseat of a car.

Andy came staggering in, weighed down by their bags and his guitar. He looked around the room. "Where's the bed?" he said, puzzled.

Debbie held up one end of the hammock with a grin.

"All right!" called Chris, hooking the hoist to the hay bale and stepping back.

Rick, standing shirtless up in the hayloft, grunted and hoisted the bale up, swinging it inside through the large square window of the loft. He pulled the bale in, unhooked it, took a deep breath, and sent the hoist back down.

"Chris, I don't understand why you guys have so much hay," he called down to her. "You don't have any horses. You never did."

Chris hooked another hay bale to the hoist and gave the rope a tug to signal him. "It was my father's idea," she shouted to him. "Every year, he makes plans to buy a horse. And every year, he buys all this hay and no horse. You figure it out."

She didn't explain that her father had actually almost bought the horse this year, but at the last minute her mother had decided that she couldn't bear to come back here again where that awful thing had happened to her daughter. And her father had never gotten around to buying the horse or canceling the hay order or any of a dozen other things that he had meant to take care of. Everything was just sort of hanging in limbo. Waiting. Just as her parents were waiting tensely at home right now, wondering how she was doing, feeling helpless and frustrated because she had refused to let them come with her and they hadn't been able to stop her from going without them. They had been astonished that she had wanted to come back here after what had happened.

Well, she hadn't *wanted* to come, but she

had no choice. And having her friends with her for the weekend, knowing she could depend upon them for support, was incredibly important. Somehow, she had to come to terms with what had happened here and learn to live with it. She couldn't very well expect her parents to do it until she could.

"You realize, of course," Rick called down to her from the loft, suddenly breaking in on her thoughts, "I gave up an opportunity to spend the weekend with Mary Jo Conrad for this."

He gave a heave on the rope.

"You mean you actually gave up a chance to be with *the* Mary Jo Conrad for little ole me?" Chris called up to him, playing along.

"That's right," he said, pulling up the next bale and swinging it inside the loft.

"Boy, are you dumb!" said Chris.

"Okay, Chris," Rick said, sending down the hoist again. "I realize I'm just a country boy and my feelings don't really matter, but this is the sweat of a worker, not a lover."

He gave a sharp pull on the rope and grunted. This was a heavy one.

"Now, I believe there's a time and place for everything," he called down to her, straining as he pulled the rope. "And now's the time and now's the place, if you know what I mean."

This hay bale seemed unusually heavy. He gritted his teeth and pulled hard, feeling the muscles bunching in his arms and shoulders. He wasn't *that* out of shape, was he?

"So what I think we should do is"—he grunted—"set aside three hours a day to fulfill our needs. One hour in the morning"—he gave another heave—"and two at night. If you agree . . ."

What the hell, he thought, straining on the rope, this hay bale seemed to weigh a ton!

Chris suddenly rose up level with him. "Were you talking to me?" she said, standing with her foot in the hoist, hanging on to the rope and giggling.

With a wry smile, Rick let go of the rope, and with yelp, Chris plummeted to the ground as the rope ran out through the block. As she hit, landing in a pile of hay and rolling, a frenzied scream came from the direction of the house.

She got up quickly and ran back toward the house. Rick climbed down from the loft and followed close behind her.

She ran up the porch steps and burst through the front door, looking all around her. There was no sign of anyone.

"Is anyone here?' she called out loudly, badly frightened by the scream.

Rick came bursting in behind her, buttoning up his shirt. "What's going on?" he said, looking around.

"I don't know," she replied tensely. "You check down here. I'll check the upstairs."

She ran up the spiral staircase to the second-floor balcony, stopped at the door to Andy and Debbie's room, and looked inside. There was no one there. No one was screaming anymore. That frightened her almost as much as the scream itself had. She bit her lower lip and continued down the corridor. She stopped at the closed door of Shelly's room.

"Is anybody there?" she called through the door.

There was no answer.

She tried the door. It was stuck. She gave it a kick and it flew open to slam against the wall inside the room.

"Shelly?"

There wasn't anyone inside, but the door to the antique armoire was slightly ajar. She approached it, pulled the door open, and screamed as Shelly's body slumped against the side of the armoire, blood glistening around a hatchet embedded in his forehead. He slid down the inside of the armoire and fell out onto the floor, his glazed eyes staring at the ceiling.

Chris recoiled from the sight and her hands came up to the sides of her face as she screamed hysterically. She felt Rick's hands on her shoulders, turning her away.

"Don't look at him!" said Rick, pulling her away. "Let's just get the hell out of here!"

Andy, Debbie, and Vera rushed into the room behind them.

"We heard screaming," said Vera.

"What's going on?" said Debbie, and then she noticed Shelly lying on the floor. "Oh, my *God!*"

Vera gasped with shock and disbelief. "What *happened?*"

Andy alone seemed unaffected. He made a face and bent down over Shelly, reaching out toward him.

"Don't move him!" Rick cautioned.

"Don't touch him!" Debbie said.

Andy placed his hands on Shelly's stomach and started tickling him. Suddenly the "corpse" started giggling uncontrollably.

"You creep!" said Andy, giving him a shot.

Shelly sat up, laughing, and removed the one-piece fake-embedded-hatchet-and-bleeding-latex-wound from his scalp. "I guess I fooled you, huh?" he said.

"Jerk!" Chris shouted. She started to pummel him furiously and Shelly covered himself up, recoiling from her anger. Rick pulled her off.

"Chris, leave him alone," said Andy disgustedly. "He doesn't know any better."

"It's a joke," said Shelly, chagrined that they were taking it that way. "It was just a joke! I didn't mean to—"

"You never mean to," Andy said.

Vera glanced at him with disdain. Christ, she thought, why do these things happen to me? I'm *never* going to let anybody fix me up with a blind date again! What a pitiful nerd!

"Oh, I gotta get out of here," she said, with exasperation. She turned to Rick. "I'm going to the store. Can I use your car?"

"Sure," said Rick, throwing her the keys and shaking his head as he looked at Shelly.

"Thanks," said Vera, turning and leaving with a disgusted look at Shelly.

"Asshole!" Chili said contemptuously, turning and shaking her head as she went out the door.

Feeling awful, Shelly sat on the floor, wiping the fake blood off his face and forehead with a handkerchief. It hadn't turned out the way he'd planned at all. He had wanted to impress them all with his creativity and his acting ability, but the joke had backfired, and instead, they all thought less of him than ever.

I wish I could die, he thought.

THREE

Vera ran down the porch steps, climbed into Rick's white VW bug, and started the engine. It caught with a cough and sputter and settled into a steady, chugging idle. She shifted into first and started to pull away when Shelly came running out of the house, waving at her.

"Hey, hey, hey!" he yelled, waving his arms and running toward the car. "Let me go with you! I gotta get outta here, too!"

Jeez, that's all I need, she thought, letting out the clutch and accelerating past him, kicking up dust as she spun around and headed for the bridge. Then she made the mistake of glancing up in the rearview mirror.

He looked so forlorn and pathetic standing there, gazing after her, that she simply couldn't help herself. Against her better judgment, she stopped the car, sighed, and opened the passenger door.

Elated, Shelly came running. I just know I'm going to regret this, she thought as he got in, beaming. She shook her head in resignation, cursing herself for being softhearted and drove off across the bridge.

"Chris! Chris, wait up!" yelled Debbie, running down the trail after her.

Chris stopped and waited for her to catch up before resuming her walk down to the lake.

"What's wrong?" said Debbie.

"Oh, it's that creep, Shelly," Chris said angrily, picking up a branch and tossing it into the bushes, as if she were throwing it at him. "What a sick sense of humor."

"Oh, that's just his way of getting attention," Debbie said. "He doesn't know about what happened."

Chris sighed with exasperation. "Oh, I know it, Deb. But from the minute we got here, I've been seeing things and hearing things . . ." She shook her head. "It's probably just my imagination. I shouldn't have come back here so soon."

"Don't let it get to you," said Debbie, trying to reassure her. "Relax. Enjoy the weekend.

Nothing's going to happen when we're all here together." She quickly tried to change the subject. "Hey, how are things going with Rick?"

"Okay," said Chris, in a resigned tone. "But he just doesn't understand." It was clear from her tone that she didn't really want to go into it.

Debbie wished that there was something she could do to make her friend feel better, to make her forget what happened, but there were some things a person simply couldn't forget. Things like what had happened to Chris last summer.

Debbie and Chris were best friends since childhood, and they had talked about it, just as Debbie had talked with Chris when she had found out that she was pregnant and had some very serious decisions to make. But what had happened that summer was the sort of thing about which Debbie couldn't really give Chris any advice. Because she didn't really know what happened. Not even Chris knew, not completely. Perhaps that was just as well, Debbie thought. On the other hand, not knowing could be even worse.

There was a dark secret buried deep in Chris's mind and there was no way of telling if she would ever be able to unearth it. Not even analysis had helped. A psychiatrist had tried to hypnotize her and cause her to regress, but she had subconsciously resisted him, refusing to go under. Chris wanted to remember, because not knowing frightened her; Debbie thought maybe there were some things that people were better off not knowing.

Chris only remembered part of what had happened to her last summer and that had been frightening enough. The rest was a complete blank. A gap that Chris felt she desperately needed to fill. But Debbie was afraid for her. After all, when the mind blocked out something so completely, there was usually a reason for it. It was self-defense.

Debbie bit her lower lip as they walked down by the lake. Chris had become silent, staring off across the water. Debbie knew that Chris was afraid of what would happen if she could never remember that missing part of her life.

But Debbie was afraid of what would happen if she did.

The cashier at the crossroads convenience store rang up the total as a local high school girl bagged their purchases—several six-packs of beer, a couple of six-packs of soda, assorted bags of chips, cookies, and a mess of candy bars, cupcakes, and doughnuts Shelly had grabbed for himself.

Vera guessed that he had used restraint because of her. Otherwise, he probably would have loaded up on two or three times as much junk food. She figured that he probably had some emergency supplies stashed away in that makeup kit of his. It was certainly big enough. She didn't even want to think about what sort of gruesome things could be inside there if that hatchet-in the-head trick was a typical example. Boy, she thought, Shelly was really strange.

"That'll be eighteen-fifty," the cashier said. "And we don't accept no food stamps."

Vera sneered at the thinly veiled racism. She thought, you wouldn't say that to an Anglo, would you, bitch? And then her face fell as she realized that she had left her wallet in her purse, which was still back at the house.

"Shelly?" she called.

He quickly put the skin mag he was leafing through back into the rack and turned around guiltily, blushing like a little boy caught doing something wrong.

"I need some money," Vera said, feeling awkward that she had to ask him.

Shelly quickly dug into the back pocket of his jeans, pulled out his cordura wallet and tossed it to her. Vera reached out to catch it, but it struck the side of her hand and fell to the floor. As she bent down to pick it up, a black leather high-heeled boot with ankle straps suddenly came down on top of it.

She looked up to see a hard-looking young black woman in skintight, black, studded motorcycle leathers standing over her. She wore a dark purple headband and lots of turquoise and silver jewelry. She backed Vera away with a hard glance, bent down, and picked up Shelly's wallet.

"*Excuse* me," Shelly said, moving toward her with his hand held out, "but I believe that's *my* wallet."

Before he could take more than three steps, Shelly was grabbed by the arms from either side and yanked up on his tiptoes. He gulped and smiled nervously at the two bikers who held him. Both wore leather vests with patches on them—large black widow spiders on the backs. One of the bikers was black, with a shaved head, a gold earring, a heavy chromed steel lock-up chain hung around his neck, and a neat little goatee that made him look satanic. The other one was white, sort of punky-looking, with short, spiky hair, shades, an earring, and a cigarette dangling from the corner of his mouth.

"Make a wish," the black guy said, grinning at the white biker as they held Shelly by the arms.

"Uh . . . could I buy you two a beer or something?" Shelly said, badly frightened but desperately trying not to show it.

The woman started going through his wallet.

"I'll take that now," said Vera, reaching out for it.

The black woman smiled and arched her eyebrows as she held up a condom in a foil packet she had found inside the wallet. "Is this your rubber?" she said.

Shelly groaned with humiliation.

Vera grabbed for the wallet, but the black woman was quick to react, pulling it back out of her reach. "Didn't your mamma teach you manners?" she said. "If you want something, you *ask. Nice!*"

Vera set her jaw, gritting her teeth.

"Please," Shelly said, "be cool . . ."

Through clenched teeth, Vera said, "May we please have the wallet . . . *ma'am?*"

"That's *good*," the black woman said. "That's *real* nice."

She slapped the wallet into Vera's outstretched hand. Vera immediately plucked a bill out of it and tossed it down onto the counter, then she snatched up their grocery bags and stormed out of the market. The punky biker flicked his cigarette butt at Shelly as they released him to run after her.

"Hey, that was a twenty!" Shelly said as he caught up to her outside in the parking lot. She hadn't even bothered with the change. Then he quickly added, "Are they following us?"

69

Vera glanced back over her shoulder. *"No,"* she snapped furiously.

"Good," Shelly said, with enormous relief. His heart had been racing back there.

Vera shoved the groceries into the backseat of the VW and tossed the keys to Shelly. "Here! *You* drive. The way I feel right now, I'd probably get us into an accident."

She got in and slammed the door.

Shelly quickly jumped into the driver's seat and inserted the keys into the ignition. "Next time, I'll know how to handle a situation like that," he said, with false bravado, as he started up the car. Then, realizing how obviously phony it sounded, he lamely added, "Let's just hope next time isn't too soon."

As the engine caught and chugged hesitantly to life, the bald biker came out of the market. He stopped to open the pop-top on a beer can and glanced up at them with a mean look.

"Uh-oh," said Vera.

Shelly swallowed nervously, quickly shifted the VW into gear, and stomped down on the gas pedal, anxious to get the hell out of there. But in his hurry to drive off, he mistakenly shifted into reverse instead of first gear and the car leaped backward with a lurch. There was the awful sound of crashing metal as the VW backed into two chopped motorcycles, knocking them both over and sending them crashing to the ground.

"Oh, *shit!*" Shelly exclaimed with horror as he realized what he had done.

"Oh, shit is right!" said Vera. "Let's get *out* of here!"

The black biker threw his beer can to the ground in a fury and raced toward them, whipping the heavy steel chain off from around his neck. Panic-stricken, Shelly slammed the gearshift lever into first and stepped on the accelerator. The car lurched forward, but the biker stood his ground, positioning himself directly in their path.

"Hold on!" yelled Shelly.

The guy's crazy, Shelly thought as he realized that the biker wasn't going to move! He hit the brakes. The car stopped inches away from the motionless biker. He leaned in close to their windshield, giving them an evil grin. And then he snarled and smashed the chain right through their windshield.

Shelly and Vera ducked, throwing their arms up to protect themselves from the flying glass. The biker wound the chain around his fist and came around the side. He hauled off and smashed the driver's side window, shattering the glass. As he pulled his fist back for another blow, this one aimed right at Shelly's face, Shelly quickly let out the clutch and the car pulled quickly away.

The biker ran over to his fallen motorcycle and bent down to pick it up, intent on giving chase.

Suddenly, Shelly made a screeching U-turn.

"What're you *doing*?" Vera said, incredulous that he had stopped and turned around when their escape was clear.

"He went too far this time!" said Shelly, closing his hands around the wheel with grim determination.

He sat hunched over, an intense expression on his face, his lips pressed tightly together, his forehead creased, his eyebrows knitted, and as the biker started to pick up his cycle, Shelly let out the clutch and floored it.

The biker couldn't believe his eyes when he saw the VW bearing down upon him. He barely managed to leap out of the way in time before Shelly ran right over his bike, purposely finishing the job he'd accidentally started. The other two bikers came running out of the store in time to see the VW pull another U-turn and slide around in a spray of dust, heading toward the road.

"I *did* it! I *did* it! *I did it!*" Shelly crowed jubilantly. "Did I do it?"

"You did it!" Vera said, with disbelief. "You were great!"

"I was great!" said Shelly, riding on the adrenaline high. It was the first time in his life he had ever stood up to anybody. It felt terrific. He glanced up into his rearview mirror.

"You son of a bitch!" the black biker yelled after him, throwing the chain after the departing car. "Come back here, you bastard! You're not gettin' away with this! I'm gonna *get* you! You're dead, you mother! You hear me? *Dead!*"

FOUR

They all came running when Shelly and Vera pulled up with the battered VW. The little car looked as if it had been through a war. The windshield was completely smashed, as well as the window on the driver's side, and there were large dents both in the front and back where Shelly had backed into the motorcycles, then run over them full-steam. As Shelly pulled up in front of the porch, Chuck reached them first. He put his hand through where the windshield used to be.

"What happened to your windshield, man?" he said.

Shelly and Vera got out of the car. "We had a slight misunderstanding with a motorcycle gang," said Shelly, trying to sound nonchalant, as if misunderstandings with motorcycle gangs were something that happened to him every day.

"Yeah, but Shelly made them see the error of their ways," said Vera, putting her arm around him. "Didn't you, Shel?"

Flustered, yet beaming with pride, Shelly managed to stammer. "It was nothing."

Rick came out and his jaw dropped when he saw what had become of his VW. "My poor car!" he said with disbelief. "What did you *do* to it?"

Vera handed him the keys as she passed him, carrying the groceries up into the house. "Yeah, well, we're really sorry, but it wasn't our fault," she said.

"A few minor repairs and it'll be as good as new," said Shelly, with a shrug, as if it were no big deal.

Rick ran up to his car and stood staring at it, shaking his head with amazement. Chris came up behind him.

"That's *it*!" said Rick, turning on her furiously. "I've *had* it! I thought it would be good for us to spend some time together, but this is a little more than I bargained for!"

He threw open the door and got into the car.

"Where are you going?" Chris said.

"Away from here," Rick said, with disgust. He didn't know what the hell he was wasting his time for. Chris didn't seem as if she wanted to pick up where they left off and he had no use whatsoever for her friends. Especially after this! He started the car.

"Stay with me," Chris said.

"Why *should* I?"

"Because I want you to," she said softly.

Rick looked up at her. She had that lost-little-girl expression on her face that he was always such a sucker for. He shook his head. "You don't play fair, do you?" he said. He took a deep breath and let it out in a heavy sigh. Then he reached across to the passenger door and opened it. "Get in."

Chris ran around to the other side and jumped into the car. Rick shifted into gear and slowly drove back down the driveway, across the wooden bridge, and out onto the road.

As they passed the dried-out streambed, a large figure dressed in grubby work clothes stepped out of the shelter of the trees. He breathed heavily as he watched the VW disappear around a bend. It was happening again. Just like the last time. These people were exactly like the others, the ones who had hurt his mother. A raging fever began to burn within him; a white-hot fire of hate threatened to consume him. And there was only one way to quench the flames.

"Hey, let's go for a swim," said Debbie, pulling on Andy's arm. All afternoon, he'd wanted to do nothing except lie around in the sun.

"I don't know ..." he said lazily, as if it would be too much of a bother to walk all the way down to the lake.

"We'd be all alone," Debbie said seductively. "We could do anything we wanted and nobody would see."

Andy grinned. "Sounds disgusting," he said. "Let's go."

"I'll grab a couple of towels," she said, smiling at him. "I'll see you down there."

She went over to the van and slid open the side door. It was really strange, but ever since she'd found out that she was pregnant, she'd been really horny. And it kept getting worse and worse. She had expected to feel positively ill. Well, there was the occasional bout with morning sickness, but other than that, she felt terrific. Chris had even commented on it. "You've got a glow," was the way she had put it.

She remembered her mother always complaining about it, always bringing it up each time they had an argument. Rolling her eyes in agony and saying, "I *carried* you for nine months! You don't have any *idea* what that's like! You should only have to experience something like that and then wind up with an ungrateful daughter!"

From listening to her mother, Debbie had expected this to be a terrible experience, but so far it was wonderful. She couldn't even tell that she was pregnant yet, at least not by looking, though she checked herself in a mirror every day, but she could feel the changes taking place inside of her. She knew the experience would not be terrible at all. It was something wonderful.

Andy was taking it in stride. The responsibility didn't seem to frighten him. He knew it would be hard for them, especially at their age, but he had simply accepted it and decided to make the best of it. A lot of guys would have freaked out, but not Andy. He stuck by her, just like she knew he would.

"The way I see it," he had told her, "the important thing is that we really *want* this baby. It's gonna be tough for us and money's gonna be real tight, but if we stick together, we can make it. We didn't plan on this, but since we've decided that we're gonna have this baby, we've got to make sure we really want it. We can't go blaming the kid if things get tough. The baby didn't make things tough for us, *we* made things tough. Now we just gotta go for it and do the best we can."

If she ever had any doubts about him, they had disappeared right then. The important thing, she thought, is that we remember the mistakes our families made with us and not make them with our kid. She knew it would be hard. But she also knew it would be worth it.

She was so preoccupied with her thoughts, she didn't hear the soft crunch of gravel beneath the heavy black engineer boots on the other side of the van. She pulled several towels out of her beach bag and zipped it back up, then trotted off toward the lake just as the punky-looking biker from the roadside convenience store slowly came around the back of the van.

He stood still for a moment, looking around with a cigarette drooping from his lip. Then he gave an animalistic grunt to signal the others that the coast was clear.

"Maybe we shouldn't do this, Ali," said Fox, the hard-looking young black woman in the skintight leathers.

"We gotta even the score, don't we?" said Loco, the white biker with the spiky hair.

"Nobody's gonna get hurt, baby," said Ali, the biker with the shaved head and goatee. He glanced at Loco and grinned. "Righteous!"

He stuck a siphon down into the fuel tank and set one of the large metal gas cans they had brought down onto the ground. Loco reached for the siphon hose.

"Let me do it," he said.

"I know what I'm doing," Ali said, backing him down with a stare.

He had to stay on top of Loco all the time. Loco was so spaced out, he'd probably wind up drinking half the gas if he let him siphon out the tank. He wasn't called Loco for nothing. That boy was truly bugfuck. He did things on that motorcycle that no sane man would ever do, and when he had seen what that fat little turd had done to his scooter, he'd been ready to do murder.

Ali just couldn't believe that fat little creep had the balls to do what he did. Luckily, Ali's bike hadn't suffered too badly. It would need a new front rim and fender, handlebars, and a replacement clutch lever, a headlight, and a few other odds and ends. He wasn't going to worry too much about the paint since they were both sort of rat bikes to begin with, and he could always do the paint himself, but Loco's machine had taken a real bashing and it would be in the shop for weeks till they could run down the parts from someone who specialized in old British bikes, since it hadn't been manufactured for years.

Loco was ready to tear that fat little bastard apart with his bare hands. He probably would, too, thought Ali, only there was no point in letting Fox know that. She acted real hard, but when it came right down to it, she was pretty soft on the inside. She was even a little squeamish about burning down the barn. Hell, the barn was gong to be only the beginning, Ali thought. Nobody trashes my scooter and gets away with it. *Nobody*.

As he siphoned the gas out of the van's tank, Fox wandered over toward the barn. There didn't seem to be anyone around, so she went inside. She could understand Ali and Loco wanting to get even with those kids for what they did, and trashing their van—or ripping it off, as she'd suggested—was one thing, but burning down a barn was getting a little heavy.

Suppose the flames got out of control and spread to the house or started a forest fire? The area was heavily wooded. Cops might not look too hard for a stolen van that was probably insured anyway and they could have it miles away before the cops could even start to look for it. Hell, she thought, by that time, the boys could have it in the shop, repainted, and the old numbers ground off, and they'd have it sold before anyone could ever trace it to them. But arson, that was something else, again.

It was that Loco, she thought. Ali was fine when he wasn't around, but when the two of them were together, Ali always had to be harder and badder and meaner, and what made it worse was that Loco simply did not know when to stop. Things could get out of hand with him really fast. She could tell he really wanted to kill those kids, and it was all her fault. If she hadn't started messing around with that Chicano girl, none of this would've happened. Well, it was out of her hands. There was nothing else to do but ride with it.

She looked around to make sure that there was no one watching and cautiously pulled open one of the barn doors. Shafts of fading sunlight cut through the gloom within, softly illuminating the straw-strewn, packed earth floor. She grinned as she looked around. It was an old barn with lots of tools and stuff stored inside it; horseshoes and old bells and blacksmith's tongs hung on the walls. A weather-worn western saddle and girth were slung over the wall of one of the two large wood-framed horse stalls with wide, swinging wooden gates. She ran her hand over the saddle. The leather was cracked and discolored.

Several wooden benches were set against the walls and a couple of old saw horses had dusty, faded woolen blankets draped over them. There was an ancient, rusty army canteen hanging from a peg, as well as an old, olive-drab, World War II canteen belt. She decided the belt looked kinda funky. She'd grab it on the way out.

It was the first time she had ever seen the inside of a barn and she felt a little like a kid turned loose in a toy store. She completely forgot about the guys outside planning to burn it down and lost herself in the fascination of rummaging through all the junk, the rusted tools, the various items of old clothing and camping equipment and worn-out riding tack that had been left hanging there. She found an old brass cowbell, struck it to hear its tone, then decided to also grab that on the way out. Then the high heel of her boot caught on something and she fell sprawling, facedown, to land with her eyes scant inches away from the upturned tines of an old pitchfork.

"Shit!" she said, realizing how close she'd come to landing right on top of the nasty-looking thing. She'd have to be more careful. You never knew what could happen to you in a dark old place like this, she thought.

She glanced up at the loft, wondering what was up there. Maybe she'd find something else that she could liberate. She took hold of the wooden ladder that extended vertically straight up to a trapdoor in the loft, and started to climb up.

Behind her, a large shadow fell across the barn floor as a massive figure came in quietly through the open door and softly pulled it shut behind him.

Ali finished filling the first gas can and quickly transferred the siphon hose to the mouth of the second can, losing only a few drops in the process. He shoved the hose down inside, then capped the first can and handed it to Loco.

"Here, take this into the bar and start pouring," he said. "And find Fox!"

That was all he needed now, having his old lady wandering off. She was probably screwin' around down by the lake, he thought, wading along the shore or some dumb thing, and here they were getting ready to torch the damn place. He wanted her where he could keep an eye on her. They'd have to hit these turkeys hard and then split fast. He didn't want anyone to be able to identify them, assuming Loco left anyone alive to do it. He was in a real state. Maybe a nice big bonfire would mellow him out, but if not, there wasn't going to be any talking him out of this one. And, bottom line, Ali didn't really feel like it. The hell with 'em. These kids had called the shots when they ran over their scooters. The sons of bitches were going to get wasted, and he wasn't going to cry about it.

Loco walked over to the barn, carrying the heavy gas can and looking all around, keeping an eye out for anyone who might give an alarm. He got over to the barn doors and set the gas can down. He was about to reach out and open up the door when a sudden shriek coming from overhead startled him, making him reach for the large folding knife in his belt sheath.

Fox came swinging out like a jungle queen on the hoist through the open square window doors of the hayloft, laughing and yelling like a kid.

"Whoooo-weeee!" she cried, with childlike delight.

Loco stared up at her in disbelief. "What the hell are you *doin'*?" he said, glancing over his shoulder quickly to see if anyone had heard her. "Are you *crazy*? Get *off* that thing!"

She disappeared from view, swinging back through the hayloft door, and a moment later she came swinging out again like a little girl in a playground on a set of swings.

"This feels so *gooooooood!*" she yelled, giggling like a child.

Loco simply stared at her. He couldn't believe it. What did the silly bitch think they were doing here, playing games for chrissake? He glanced back over his shoulder, looking in Ali's direction. The van was out of sight, around a bend in the driveway, behind a large oak tree. He shook his head. If Ali saw this, he'd lose it for damn sure.

"Ali's gonna be pissed if you don't stop this screwin' around!" he called up to her. "We got shit to do!"

The hoist came swinging out by itself, with no sign of Fox.

Loco waited for a moment, staring up at the hayloft, but Fox didn't reappear. He scowled and went into the barn.

"Fox!" he called, getting really irritated. He wanted to get on with it; he didn't feel like wasting time playing nursemaid to Ali's old lady. "Where *are* ya?"

The cigarette dangled from his mouth. I oughta just dump the goddamn gas out and toss the butt down and be done with it, he thought. Let the stupid bitch find her own way out. Serve her right if she got burned. He ground his teeth together. No, then he'd have to deal with Ali. Where's Fox? he imagined Ali saying. Oh, she's back in the barn, man. Oughta be nice and crispy by now. No, he didn't guess Ali would go for that. Shit. He'd better get her and bring her the hell out.

"Stop screwin' around!" he yelled up at the loft. "You're messin' everything up!"

There was no response.

"Shit," he said savagely, staring up the ladder to the hayloft. He'd had it with her. He didn't care if she was Ali's old lady or not, he was going to grab her by her goddamn throat and toss her right out that big square window up there. "You're *dead* now, woman!" he shouted.

He came up through the opening in the floor and stepped off the ladder onto the floorboards.

"Fox!"

He turned around . . . his jaw dropped and his eyes opened wide with shock at the sight of Fox dangling in the air, pinned to a crossbeam, impaled through the throat by the long tines of a pitchfork like a butterfly pinned to a board. Her eyes were ghastly, wide open, frozen into a stare of utter horror. Blood trickled down her leathers and dripped down onto the floor of the loft, soaking into the straw.

Loco panicked and turned to run.

The second pitchfork was driven deep into his stomach with a dull, wet, smacking sound; the long, sharp tines ripped through his entrails, penetrating deeply, going straight through him and coming out his back. Blood bubbled up into his throat as he opened his mouth to scream, and his hands clutched helplessly at the wooden shaft of the pitchfork, his horrified gaze fixed on his attacker. He staggered forward one step, and then his legs turned to rubber and collapsed beneath him. There was a brief period of the most incredible, agonizing pain he had ever experienced in his entire life, and then everything started spinning and he was falling as fire exploded in his mind and the whole world started burning.

Ali came hurrying up to the barn doors, carrying a heavy can of gasoline in each hand. He scowled at the sight of the closed doors and kicked at them, looking around to see if anyone had heard him. He waited for either Fox or Loco to let him in, but no one came. Angrily, he kicked the door again.

"Loco! Fox! *Open this damn door!*"

There was no response from inside. Ali gritted his teeth and set the gas cans down, then pushed the door open himself. He picked up the cans and went inside, setting them down once again and looking all around the interior of the barn. They were nowhere in sight. He heard the sound of heavy footsteps up in the hayloft and looked up.

"What the hell are you two doin' up there?" he demanded angrily. "You hear me talkin' to you?"

He stormed over to the ladder and grabbed it, about to start climbing up, when suddenly Loco's body was thrown down from the hayloft. It came flying down at Ali, landing right on top of him and sending him crashing to the ground. His eyes went wide as he saw all the blood and he shoved Loco's corpse away, scrambling out from under it.

"FOX!" he screamed, and then he turned quickly as someone dropped down from the hayloft, landing back in a dark corner of the barn.

Ali looked around quickly and his gaze fell on a rusted machete among the array of gardening tools. He grabbed it and started for the back of the barn, his eyes glittering with homicidal fury.

"When I find you, you bastard, you're a *dead man!*" he said.

He rushed back to the stalls, brandishing the machete, and then he spun quickly as he heard someone jump down behind him from the pile of hay bales in the corner. In the dim light inside the barn, he saw a huge figure coming at him, holding something in his hand. Ali swung the machete at the shadowy figure's head with all his might.

Moving with amazing speed, his attacker ducked beneath the blow and Ali staggered, momentarily caught off balance, and then stars burst before his eyes as an iron plumber's wrench came down upon his skull and he fell crashing to the floor. The wrench descended on him three more times like a sledgehammer driving in a railroad spike, but Ali never felt it.

FIVE

He saw them through the window of the barn, the girl dressed in a scanty blue bikini and wrapped in a towel, the boy in shorts, sneakers, and a T-shirt. Their wet hair was plastered down and they walked close to one another, hand in hand. They were coming up from the boat dock by the lake, heading directly toward the barn. Their voices floated up to him.

"What're you doing?" Debbie said as Andy started to pull her toward the barn.

"We haven't been in the barn yet," Andy said, with a sly grin. "Let's take a look."

"Not now," said Debbie, pulling away from him and walking back toward the house. "I'm cold." The water in the lake was freezing and it had brought on a sudden attack of cramps and mild nausea.

"How about it, Debbie?" Andy said, wiggling his eyebrows and leering. "A little roll in the hay?"

"Go play with yourself," she said, grinning at him. "I'm going in the house."

"Hey, wait up!" he yelled, laughing and running after her.

Jason Vorhees slowly unclenched his fists as the couple headed back up toward the house. The bloodstained plumber's wrench dropped from his hand and fell onto the floor of the barn, next to the prostrate form of Ali. He looked down at the biker's blood-spattered body and, for a moment, the raging fever within him ebbed. His breathing slowed and became more regular. A curious sort of calm came over him, as it always did after a kill. But it only lasted for a little while, and each time the period of calm was briefer than the last.

He had fled from the deserted Camp Crystal Lake—known to the locals as "Camp Blood"—after the sheriff, with assistance from local hunters and the state police, had organized a search for him. It was the largest dragnet in the history of the state. They had started at Paul Holt's counselor training center, the scene of the recent murders, and from there they had gone on to the abandoned camp, where they had found the ruined, patched-together cabin he'd been living in. From hiding, he had watched them carrying out the bodies of the counselors he had slain and brought them to the shrine he had erected to his mother, the centerpiece of which had been her rotting, decapitated head. It was all that remained of her after the girl named Alice, the sole survivor of her vengeance, had killed her at the camp, beheading her with a machete.

Thinking he had drowned and blaming his death on inattentive counselors, Pamela Vorhees had been driven mad with grief and she had embarked upon a murderous vendetta to avenge her son. She butchered two young counselors while they were making love, savagely hacked them to pieces with a hunting knife so that their bodies were barely recognizable. Then she had poisoned the camp water supply. Each time someone tried to open up the camp again, she stopped them until Steve Christy, the son of the original owner, returned with a setup crew of counselors, determined to reopen the camp and prove once and for all that "Camp Blood" wasn't cursed, as people in the town of Crystal Lake believed. Enraged, she killed them all, except for Alice, who, in terrified desperation, struck out at her with a machete and ended her pathetic life. Only what Pamela

Vorhees had never realized was that her son, Jason, had survived.

Jason *had* drowned in Crystal Lake on that fateful Friday the 13th, but some feral spark within him had refused to die. He had come to on the shore, with no memory of how he had dragged himself up out of the slime at the bottom of the lake. The last thing he remembered was crying out in terror as the waters of the lake closed over him, the awful feeling of the water rushing down his throat, flooding his lungs as he tried uselessly to breathe ... and then nothing.

When he found himself in a clump of bushes on the shore he rolled over on his side and retched for what seemed like hours, vomiting up filthy, stagnant water, worms, and writhing maggots. After a time, he regained enough strength to crawl a short distance from the lake and collapse beneath a stand of pine trees, where he slept while his body continued the strange process of regeneration that had kept it alive despite all the rules of nature.

He did not know how much time had passed since he had drowned, how *long* he had remained on the bottom of the lake, but even had he known, chances were he would not have understood. The ordeal of his "death" had dealt an irreparable blow to his tortured mind, which had never really functioned properly to start with. Despite the supernatural ability of his body to shut down and repair itself, his mind was never fully able to recover from the effects of brain death. He lived, but he did not really reason. He was a human shark, motivated by nothing more complicated than a relentless urge to kill.

He had avenged his mother's death, then returned to the abandoned camp on the shore of Crystal Lake to carry on her grisly work. And when Paul Holt had come to open his camp counselor training center on the lakeshore near the abandoned summer camp, Jason had killed them all, save for Ginny Field, who had survived miraculously after he left her for dead. When they came with dogs and rifles to hunt him, he fled deep into the woods, then plunged into a stream and followed its course, causing the dogs to lose the scent while he doubled back to the lake and worked his way around the searchers. Instinctively, he outmaneuvered them and did the last thing they expected him to do. He returned to Crystal Lake.

They expected him to flee deeper and deeper into the woods, heading for high ground. They would never think to look for him on the north side of the lake, closer to the town, where there was the thickest concentration of summer homes and vacation cabins. By keeping to rocky ground and then wading through the stream which fed the lake, he left no tracks for them to follow. When it grew dark, they gave up their search.

And then he started to hunt.

Rick parked the battered Volkswagen just off the road overlooking a quiet cove, about twenty-five yards from the water. He switched off the radio seconds before the announcer came on with a special bulletin updating the progress of the manhunt for "The Camp Blood Killer." There was no television in the cabin and none of them had been listening to the radio since they arrived. So far, they hadn't heard a thing about it.

He turned the engine off, left the headlights on, then got out of the car and walked with Chris down to the water's edge. They sat down on a log and looked out over the water, which gleamed with the reflection of the moonlight and the beams from the car's headlamps. When Chris rubbed her shoulders because she felt chilly, Rick took off his denim jacket and draped it around her.

"Is that better?" he said, moving close to her.

She smiled at him in a distracted manner. He picked up a few pebbles and tossed them one by one into the water. He glanced at Chris after a few moments. She seemed a thousand miles away. He suddenly wanted very much to take her in his arms and kiss her, but as he put his arm around her, he felt her body tense. He sighed and took his arm away. He knew something was bothering her, but he couldn't figure out what the hell it was. Was it something he had done or failed to do? Something had really changed between them since last summer. Maybe there was someone else back home, he thought. But surely, if that were the case, she would have told him.

"You know, I don't think I could live anywhere else," he said, looking out at the lake and just talking to make conversation, hoping he could get her to open up. "The nights are always so peaceful and quiet."

She didn't say anything for a moment, then, still not looking at him, she said softly, "It's deceiving."

He glanced at her sharply, puzzled by the peculiar comment. "What do you mean?"

Again, she was silent for a moment, as if she were struggling to get the words out. "The quiet can fool you," she said finally. He saw her swallow hard. "It fooled me."

Rick sensed that she was on the verge of telling him about it, whatever it was, but she was having a difficult time of it. Suddenly he didn't think it was another guy back home. It was something worse. Something was really bothering her. Something had happened and she was scared.

"Chris," he said, gently prompting her, "why did you come back here?"

She hesitated, moistening her lips. Her mouth had gone suddenly dry. "To prove something to myself," she said at last. "To prove I'm stronger than I think I am."

"What about us?" Rick said.

"I'm here with you," she said, looking at him intently. "Can't that be enough for now?"

"I don't know," said Rick, his frustration mounting. She seemed about to tell him, but suddenly she backed off again. "I mean, I don't see you for months on end, and when I do, you put this barrier between us. How do I break through?"

She sighed heavily. "You're right," she said. "I should have told you everything a long time ago, but I just couldn't." She bit her lower lip and shook her head, looking away from him. She looked as if she was about to cry.

"Look, Chris," he said, "you don't have to tell me anything if you don't want to."

"I want to," she said, looking at him earnestly. "I want you to know what happened so you'll understand."

She looked away from him and stared out at the water. She was afraid to tell him, afraid that he wouldn't understand, but she could not go on any longer without telling him about it. It wasn't fair. She owed him at least that much.

"Everything is so clear in my mind," she said, "as if it were happening right now." She shut her eyes a moment, taking a deep breath and letting it out slowly. "I don't know if you remember," she said, "but when you dropped me off that night, it was very late. I knew my parents would be waiting up for me. But I didn't care. We'd had such a good time."

She sighed again and looked at him briefly before looking away once more. He was watching her intently, allowing her to proceed at her own pace, just listening and not commenting. He was dong his best to make it easier for her. Maybe he really *would* understand, she thought. Maybe he won't blame *me,* as my parents did. The thought made it a little easier for her to go on. Now that she had started, she had to tell the whole story and it simply came spilling out of her.

"The minute I got in the door," she said, "they started yelling at me and cursing me. We had such a big fight. My mom slapped me. That was the first time my mother had ever hit me. I couldn't believe it. I ran out the door and into the woods. I wanted to punish them. I decided to hide out all night. I'd get them so worried that they'd be sorry for what they did."

Her voice caught and she took another deep breath, trying to steady her nerves. Talking about it was bringing it vividly into focus. Rick took hold of her hand and gave it a reassuring squeeze. She continued.

"It had been raining out and the woods were cold and wet. I found a dry spot under an oak tree and I guess I fell asleep. All I can remember next is being startled out of sleep by the sound of footsteps. I was sure it was Dad, so I sat up and listened for him."

She began to tremble.

"The footsteps stopped," she said, her heart beating faster as she relived it in her mind. Her mouth felt dry. Her skin was clammy. "Then I heard this crackling noise behind me. I turned around and standing there was this hideous-looking man . . . so grotesque he was almost inhuman. He . . he had a knife and . . . and he attacked me with it!"

Tears started down her face as she gripped Rick's hand with a fierce intensity but avoided looking at him. She felt herself shaking and she fought to keep her voice steady. I've got to tell it, she thought desperately, I've *got* to, this is part of it, I've got to face what happened. . . .

"I . . . I was so hysterical, I don't know how I was even able to think," she said, her voice trembling as she blinked back the tears, but they were running freely now, making long, moist trails down her cheeks. "But I kicked the knife out of his hands and I ran." She gulped, forcing herself to go on. "But he ran after me and pulled me down to the ground. I was kicking and screaming, but it didn't do any good. Then ... oh, God ... then he dragged me by the hair along the ground ... And I ... I blacked out ... I just don't know what happened after that. I-just-don't-*know!*"

She broke down, sobbing uncontrollably, burying her face in Rick's shoulder as he gently pulled her close and stroked her hair. He had an agonized expression on his face as he understood for the first time why she had stiffened every time he tried to touch her, what it must have been like for her to be assaulted like that and not know what had happened, suspecting the awful truth, wanting to know and, at the same time, being terrified of knowing.

"It's all right," he said softly, stroking her hair gently, feeling her pain. "You're all right now."

He held her until she cried herself out and pulled away, taking deep breaths as she tried to calm herself. She wiped her eyes and smiled at him weakly, grateful beyond words for his understanding.

"When I woke up, I was in my own bed," she continued, holding on to his hands. She shook her head. "My parents never said a word about it. They act as if the whole thing never happened. But it did."

And they knew it too, she thought, and they

blamed her for it and never forgave her, either. They acted as though what *she* put them through—which was, of course, the way they would have thought of it—could possibly compare with an experience as terrible as the one she'd had, so terrible that her mind had blocked it out.

"All I want to do is just forget it," she said, but I *can't*. I'll never forget that horrible face! *Never!*"

The headlights on the car suddenly went out and she jerked as if struck.

"What's that?"

They turned around, looking back toward the car, but there wasn't anyone in sight.

"Damn it, it's the battery," Rick said. "I charged it yesterday, but it must not have taken."

They walked back to the car.

"It may just start anyway," he said, somewhat dubiously. "Let me try."

He opened the door, got in, and turned the key, but it was dead as a doornail.

"We're gonna have to walk back," he said, getting out and putting his arm around her protectively. "It's okay."

He looked at her and could see that she was shaken, but her eyes were shining and she looked incredibly relieved. It suddenly occurred to him that she had been afraid he'd pull away from her, afraid that he wouldn't understand and that he'd shut her out after he found out what had happened, as if it were *her* fault that some sick bastard had . . . My God, he thought, no *wonder* she'd been acting that way! No wonder she had reacted that way every time he tried to touch her! She had been violated and the assault had been upon the very core of her being. She felt unclean and was terrified that he would perceive her that way and want nothing more to do with her! Sweet Jesus, he thought, did she really think I'd turn my back on her just because she had been hurt? Did she really think I wouldn't be there when she needed me the most?

Perhaps it was a corny gesture, but he offered her his arm. And it was exactly the right thing to do. With a smile, she hooked her arm through his and together they started back down the road.

SIX

Chuck and Chili were slumped in identical postures on the couch, heads arched back, mouths open, dead to the world. "Zonked," as Chuck would have put it. Vera and Debbie sat on the other couch staring with bored expressions at Andy and Shelly, who were juggling. Shelly was juggling three apples while Andy juggled oranges, each concentrating intensely as he attempted to outdo the other. Neither Debbie nor Vera could believe that the evening had degenerated to such a mundane level.

"Do you give up?" said Shelly, concentrating fiercely as he juggled his apples.

"Not on your life!" said Andy, whose competitive drive led him to enter any physical contest, no matter how absurd. "You give up?"

"Never!" Shelly said.

Vera and Debbie exchanged helpless glances.

"I know how to stop this," Debbie said, smiling.

She got up off the couch and walked slowly over to Andy's side, stopping right next to him and sliding up to him as he kept his eyes on the oranges.

"I can think of much better things for you to be doing with your hands," she said in a husky voice, smiling and sashaying over to the stairs. Andy promptly allowed the oranges to drop.

"You win," he said to Shelly as his oranges thudded to the floor and he hastened to follow Debbie up the stairs.

Shelly glanced around, saw that Andy and Debbie had departed and that Chuck and Chili were still asleep, then he looked at Vera nervously and smiled. "I guess that just leaves you and me . . . sort of," he added, awkwardly.

Vera watched him juggle. "You really are very good at that," she said, anxious to change the subject.

She turned back to tend the fire with the poker. Shelly stopped juggling his apples and watched her for a moment, licking his lips nervously as he saw the way her jeans stretched tightly over her ass. God, she was so damned beautiful. . . . . He look a deep breath and decided to take the plunge.

"Vera . . ." he started, hesitantly, "you and I have gotten to know each other a little today." He gulped. "I like you. I like you a lot. I . . . I was thinking that maybe. . . ."

Vera came up to him quickly and gently placed her hand upon his mouth, covering his lips with the tips of her fingers. "I don't think so," she said, trying to say it as gently as she knew how.

Shelly dropped his gaze to the floor, feeling his face burning with embarrassment. He felt like an idiot.

"Look," said Vera, feeling sorry for him, "I'm going outside for a few minutes. And when I get back, we'll talk, okay?"

She turned and walked out the front door, onto the porch. Shelly moved over to the living-room window and watched her for a moment as she sat down on the porch steps.

"Sure, we'll talk," he said, a world of bitterness in his voice stemming from a lifetime of rejection. "Bitch."

Vera ambled down the porch steps to the front walk leading to the driveway. The sun had gone down and the night was cool. She took a deep breath and sighed, unaware that Shelly was watching her with desperate longing through the living-room window. He really wasn't a bad guy, she thought, even if he was a bit of a nerd. He'd shown a lot of guts at that convenience store with the bikers. Still, she thought, just because he wasn't a bad guy was no reason for her to give in to what was obviously a fairly potent sexual fantasy he was having about her.

What was it about guys, she thought, that they couldn't seem to think about girls in any other terms except as potential sexual conquests? They either wanted to take you to bed or they didn't. That's all there was to it so far as they seemed to be concerned. Friendship? Forget it. That's what other guys were for, right? When it came to women, guys either wanted to ball them or they didn't and girls would either put out or they wouldn't. It really didn't seem to be any more complex than that. How the hell could they expect to have relationships with women if they weren't even willing to accept women as individuals, with wants and needs and feelings of their own?

Damn it, she thought, I *like* Shelly. At heart, he really is a decent sort of guy, but why do I have to feel guilty just because I don't want to sleep with him? Why does my acceptance or rejection of him have to come down to whether or not I'll go to bed with him? That's just not *fair,* she thought.

Maybe she could explain it to him. She didn't know if he would understand, but it was certainly worth a try. Look, Shelly, she imagined herself saying to him, just because I don't want to go to bed with you doesn't mean that I don't like you as a person. It doesn't mean that I'm rejecting you. Don't you see that by putting me in that position, you're putting me in the same unfair position that people have been putting *you* in all your life? They've looked at you and seen a kid who was overweight and they never bothered to look beyond that to find out who you really were. Well, it can be exactly like that for someone who looks the way I do. Have you ever thought of that? They look at me and all they see is a pretty face and a terrific body. Not that I'm complaining, but there's a lot more to what I am than great legs, a tight ass, and nice tits. Just as there's a lot more to what *you* are than chubby cheeks and love handles. You'd like me to see that, to recognize that there's more to you than what you look like on the outside, but at the same time, you don't seem to be willing to give me that same consideration!

When you look at me, Shelly, she imagined herself saying to him, what do you see? My pretty face? My tits? My legs? My ass? Do you think about who I really am, or do you think about what's between my legs? What do you really *know* about me, anyway? Can't you see that you're victimizing me the same way people have been victimizing you? You *like* the way that feels? No? Then why are you doing it to *me*?

She sighed and continued walking down the path leading to the lake. The male thing was especially hard for a young Hispanic woman. She had to deal with the whole Latino macho trip. In order to preserve her virtue, her desirability as a potential mate, she had to be a virgin. Yet, at the same time, she was subjected to countless assaults upon her virginity, and the rules of the game were clearly defined. It was all right for the guys to do whatever was necessary—short of outright rape—to try and get between her legs, but the only way that she could maintain their respect was to continue to resist them. If she relented and gave them what they wanted, she would be regarded as nothing more than a cheap slut. Anglos pulled the same kind of number, only in a much more subtle way.

Maybe she was expecting too much of Shelly to think that he could ever understand. He was probably in there right now, feeling sorry for himself and thinking that she was a bitch because she wouldn't respond to him the way he wanted. And what about what *she* wanted? Or didn't that matter? She felt like going in there and asking him if he'd still feel the same way if she were about fifty pounds heavier. Somehow, she doubted he'd look at her quite the same way then. Well, Shelly, she thought, it works both ways, you know.

Andy rolled from side to side experimentally in the net hammock, feeling it sway beneath him. There was a dubious expression on his face as he looked up at Debbie, standing over him.

"How do we do it?" he said.

"Well, first we take off our clothes," she said, with a perfectly straight face, "then you get on top of me or I get on top of you."

He grimaced wryly. "I *know* how to do it. I mean, how do we do it in a *hammock*?"

With a sly smile, Debbie removed her blouse. "I think you can figure something out," she said.

"I'll think of something," Andy said as she came into his arms and the hammock started to sway from side to side.

Chuck stirred groggily on the couch in the living room. He glanced over at Chili, out like a light as she sprawled back against the couch next to him. He grinned. Good shit, man, he thought. It zonked both of us right out. He glanced around the room. Except for him and Chili, there was nobody else around. The room was dark and the fire was starting to die down. Stretching lazily, he got up off the couch, threw some more logs onto the fire, and went out the back door. He walked the short distance to the outhouse, opened the door, and pulled the light chain inside. The yellow bulb came on, and he looked around at the interior of the outhouse, grinning at the graffiti written on the walls. HELP! I'M BEING HELD PRISONER IN THE OUTHOUSE, one said. THROW DOWN A CAN OF AIR FRESHENER AND A ROPE! He chuckled, then turned around as he heard the sound of footsteps on the gravel behind him.

"Shelly?"

No answer.

He couldn't see very far in the darkness. He shrugged, went into the outhouse, closed the door, and sat down. He pulled a joint out of his shirt pocket and lit up, inhaling deeply. As the first blast hit his lungs, the whole outhouse seemed to shake.

"Heavy shit!" he said, taking the joint out of his mouth and gazing at it appreciatively.

Then the outhouse shook again and he realized that it wasn't the dope. Someone was leaning on the outhouse wall outside, rocking it back and forth violently.

"Who's there?" Chuck shouted, feeling slightly alarmed. "Shelly, if this is another one of your tricks . . ."

A moment later, he was pulling up his pants and bolting out the door, looking all around angrily. There was no sign of anyone, but the door to the barn was slowly swinging closed, as if someone had just gone inside. Damn that Shelly, Chuck thought, him and his constant screwing around. Suddenly he turned and almost jumped out of his skin when he bumped right into Chili. He gave out a startled yell.

"*Aaah!*"

"It's just me!" she said.

Chuck exhaled heavily. "Between you and Shelly, I'm lucky I haven't had a heart attack already!"

"What's butterball up to now?" asked Chili.

"I don't know," said Chuck. "He just ducked into the barn."

Chili grinned. "Come on, let's give him some of his own medicine."

She took his arm and pulled him toward the barn. As they entered the dark building, every shadowy form within suddenly looked ominous to Chuck. He started to get an attack of paranoia.

"I don't think he's in here," he said uneasily, backing away slowly toward the door.

Chili made a face and grabbed his arm, pulling him back in. Chuck suddenly wasn't sure that it was Shelly who had gone into the barn. He hadn't actually seen him. . . .

"Hey, maybe that *wasn't* him, Chili . . ." he said nervously.

"Sssh!" She held a finger to her lips, and with her other hand, she picked up an iron crowbar. She crept forward and pushed open one of the stalls.

She brought the bar up as if it were a baseball bat and leaped into the stall with shrill yell. But the stall was empty and she dropped the bar, disappointed that Shelly wasn't there.

"I guess he must've left," she said, with a shrug.

"Come on," said Chuck, anxious to get out of there. He didn't know why, but he had a sudden powerful feeling that they were not alone. He half expected someone—or some *thing*—to come leaping out at them from the shadows. "Let's get *out* of here!" he urged her.

She turned and smiled at the frightened expression on his face. She put her arm around him and hugged him close. "I'm not going to let anybody hurt you," she said.

"Gee, thanks," said Chuck wryly. "I feel a lot better."

As they turned and went outside, their arms around each other, the gate to the second stall inside the barn swung open and Jason stepped out, watching them with glittering eyes. The blood was pounding in his ears, filling them with a roaring sound as he kept clenching and unclenching his fists. His massive rib cage rose and fell as he breathed heavily, gulping in deep lungfuls of air to try and ease the tightness in his chest. The blood fever was upon him once again. He seemed to hear a small, insistent voice deep within his twisted brain, a voice that commanded him to kill. He stared at Chuck and Chili with utter loathing as they walked back toward the house. For the moment, they had escaped him.

But only for the moment.

SEVEN

Vera sat on the edge of the boat dock, dangling her legs in the water. It was so quiet and peaceful out on the lake, she didn't really feel like going back inside and having it out with Shelly. She sighed. Why couldn't he simply take the hint? Any other guy would have realized long ago that she simply wasn't interested in him, at least not *that* way, but Shelly couldn't seem to get it through his head. He kept trying to push the issue, as if he thrived on rejection.

She kicked her legs back and forth, enjoying the feel of the cool water on her bare feet. I came on this trip to get away from hassles, she thought, to just enjoy a quiet weekend in the woods. She didn't need this crap from Shelly. He wouldn't be such a bad guy, she thought, if he would just relax and stop trying to show off and impress people, if he would just be himself. Why couldn't he just . . .

Something grabbed hold of her leg.

She gasped, lurching forward, almost falling off the dock into the lake as a hand sticking up out of the water clutched her around the ankle, trying to pull her down. She screamed and clung to the dock with all her might, kicking with her leg, trying to wrench herself loose, but she felt herself slipping . . . and suddenly the hand let go.

As she scrambled panic-stricken back onto the dock, looking fearfully down into the water, a large figure in a black wet suit broke the surface of the water with a loud cry, brandishing a spear gun and wearing a white plastic hockey mask. Shelly pushed the mask back on his head and grinned at her.

"You've just learned a valuable lesson," he said as she stared at him with stunned disbelief. "A beautiful girl like you should never go out in the dark alone."

"*Damn* it, Shelly!"

She came at him furiously, meaning to strike him. But seeing the expression on her face, Shelly quickly backed away.

"*Why* do you do these stupid things," she said, in exasperation.

"I have to," he replied defensively, raising his arms slightly as if to ward off a blow.

"No, you don't *have to*," she said, making a face at him and mimicking his tone.

"I just want you to like me," Shelly said dejectedly, avoiding her gaze and looking like a dog that had been kicked.

"I *do* like you," said Vera, with exasperation. "But not when you act like a *jerk*."

"Being a jerk is better than being a nothing," Shelly said, in a small voice.

"I never said you were nothing," Vera protested.

"You don't have to say it," he said miserably. "I can tell."

"You're wrong," she said. "Shelly . . ."

He hung his head and walked away, looking like a big black seal in his wet suit. She sighed, shaking her head. God, he was truly hopeless, she thought. He acted like an insecure twelve-year-old who would do anything for attention. Like the boys who used to chase her all the time when she was a little girl. They teased her, pulled her hair, and acted like utter idiots around her because it was the only way they knew how to show they liked her. He was making her crazy. She went back to the end of the dock and sat down again, staring out at the lake and wondering if she was going to survive this weekend.

* * *

Shelly sat down on the porch swing and stared down at the dock, where Vera was sitting with her back to him. He felt like a jerk. She's right, he thought miserably, a jerk is exactly what I am.

The idea had been to make her laugh, but it had backfired, as his ideas always did. He would imagine the whole thing in his head, the way it would go, complete with dialogue, as if it were a movie that he was directing. He would see it played out in his mind frame for frame. He would leap up out of the water in his mask and wet suit, Vera leaping back, frightened at first, then amused at the stunt and flattered by the trouble he had gone to on her account—but, of course, that was not how it turned out. These things never turned out the way he imagined they would.

Shelly sighed heavily. I give up, he thought. What's wrong with me, anyway? Why can't I ever do anything right? I ought to just give up on the whole thing, forget about Vera, forget about a career in filmmaking, and get a job as a cook at a fast-food restaurant. The thought suddenly made him long for a double burger, a quarter pounder with cheese, a couple of orders of large fries, a large milkshake, and maybe a fried fish fillet with extra sauce and an apple turnover. He wondered if there were any fast-food places nearby. Or at least a pizzeria. He was starving.

A shadow crossed one of the windows and he glanced up to see who it was, but the figure had already passed. Whoever it was had gone around the house, heading toward the barn. Shelly got off the porch swing and went down the steps toward the barn, carrying his mask and spear gun. He went up to the window and looked in, but it was way too dark to see anything. He tapped on the window.

"Chuck? Chili? What're you guys doin' in there?" He grinned. "You guys doin' something I shouldn't see?"

He pushed open the door and fumbled for the light switch. Powerful fingers suddenly closed around his wrist in a vise-like grip and brutally yanked him forward. He gasped with shocked surprise, then he saw a flash of steel and opened his mouth to scream, but he never had the chance. The knife blade whistled through the air with the speed of a Japanese chef slicing up a stir fry, and Shelly felt the agonizing fire of its razor-sharp edge as it slashed across his throat.

Vera shifted uncomfortably on the wooden boards of the dock and reached into her back pocket to see what was poking her. She pulled out Shelly's wallet. She had forgotten to give it back to him after that scene with the bikers at the convenience store. Out of curiosity, she opened it and started going through the contents. She paused at a photograph of Shelly and his mother and guiltily closed the wallet. She looked around, but he was nowhere in sight. He must have gone back to the house, she thought. She started to get up, but as she rose, the wallet slipped out of her grasp and fell into the water.

"Oh, that's just great," she said, looking down at the wallet floating in the lake.

Fortunately, it was one of those cordura nylon outdoorsman's wallets, used by fisherman and boaters because they floated, but it had drifted out of her reach and now she couldn't get at it from the dock. There was nothing else to do but go in after it.

She walked back to the opposite end of the dock and stepped onto the ground, going down to the water's edge. Slowly wading out into the water until it was up over her knees, she reached out for the floating wallet and picked it up. As she shook it off, the sound of heavy footsteps on the dock above her made her look up.

She saw a dark figure wearing a white hockey mask and carrying a spear gun walk out onto the dock. Shelly, she thought, was still playing his stupid games. Well, he probably wouldn't think it was so funny when he found out she had dropped his wallet in the water. Everything inside was soaking wet.

"Hey ... I dropped your wallet!" she called out. "I'm sorry!"

She saw him raise the spear gun.

"Hey, now cut that out!" she shouted. "That's not funny!"

It was pointed straight at her. Suddenly she realized that the dark figure wasn't wearing a wet suit. It wasn't Shelly, but a much larger man, some huge and frightening stranger wearing Shelly's hockey mask and aiming Shelly's spear gun directly at her face. . . .

"Who are you?" she shouted, staring with sudden fear at the figure on the dock. *"What are you doing?"*

Jason pulled the trigger. With a click and a sharp, hissing sound, the steel spear hurtled through the air and struck Vera in her left eye, penetrating deep into her brain. She fell back into the water, her right eye staring blindly at the sky, the shiny spear shaft protruding from her left eye socket as blood leaked out from around the window and mingled with the cold waters of Crystal Lake.

Jason dropped the spear gun onto the dock and turned back toward the house. He looked up at the light in a second-floor bedroom window, where Andy and Debbie lay wrapped in each others arms.

"That was the best one yet," said Debbie, sighing contentedly. "Was it you . . . me . . . or the hammock?"

"I vote for me," said Andy, with a grin.

"I vote for the hammock," she said, giggling as she sat up and lowered her feet to the floor. She stood and reached for her bathrobe.

"Where are you goin'?" Andy said.

"I'm taking a shower," she said, pausing at the door. "You ought to try it sometime."

She went into the bathroom, flicked on the light switch, and turned on the shower.

"Hey, Debbie, can you hear me?" Andy shouted from outside the bathroom door.

She dropped her bathrobe to the floor. "Barely," she said.

"I'm going downstairs to get a brew," he called, "You want one?"

She got into the shower and started soaping herself. Downstairs, the front door opened and Jason walked in, carrying a machete from the barn. He slowly crossed the living room and started up the spiral staircase to the second floor, and the sound of their voices.

As Debbie washed the soap out of her eyes, the door to the bathroom opened. She heard a banging noise and turned off the shower.

"Andy?"

She wiped the water out of her eyes and opened them. She could see a shadowy figure through the shower curtain. She drew the curtain back and saw Andy, upside down, walking on his hands. The banging sound had been him kicking the bathroom door open. She rolled her eyes at him.

He came down out of his handstand, grinning, "Do you want that beer, or not?"

"Sure."

"I'll be right back," said Andy. He kicked up into a handstand once again and walked out of the bathroom on his hands. Smiling, Debbie shook her head and pulled the shower curtain closed. He was always showing off. She turned the hot water back on.

Andy kept his balance perfectly as he walked on his hands into the hall, whistling to himself. One of these days, he thought, I'll have to see if I've got enough nerve to try this going down the stairs. Wonder if I can make it without getting killed?"

"Andy . . ." Debbie called out from the bathroom over the sound of running water. "Are you still out there?"

He stopped and pivoted around on his hands . . . and found himself looking at a pair of dirty work boots. He glanced up and saw a large figure wearing a white hockey mask and brandishing a gleaming machete. He screamed as the razor-sharp blade chopped down savagely between his legs, slicing through his upside-down body like an ax splitting logs.

Over the sound of the running water, Debbie thought she heard a yell, followed by a crashing sound. She finished rinsing off the soap, turned off the water, and stepped out of the shower.

"Andy?" she called, reaching for a towel. "Are you still out there? I can't hear you! Will you quit fooling around? Cut it out!"

She dried off, then wrapped the towel around herself and opened the bathroom door. She stuck her head out and looked up and down the hall, but there was no sign of him. He must've gone downstairs, she thought.

"I changed my mind, I don't want that beer!" she shouted, looking down over the balcony as she walked down the hall to their bedroom, her bare feet almost stepping into a trail of blood. "Andy? *Andy?* Did you hear me about that beer?"

She stopped at the bedroom door, listening for a moment, then sighed with exasperation and went inside. "I hate when you don't answer!" she said, slamming the door shut and plopping down into the hammock. She reached over to the nightstand, picked up a magazine, and settled herself down comfortably, flipping through the pages while she waited for him to return.

With a soft, pattering sound, several large drops of blood fell down from above and splattered on the pages of her magazine.

Not realizing what it was at first, Debbie frowned and touched the red drops with her fingertips. *"Where's this coming from?"* she wondered aloud. Then she looked up and saw Andy's mangled body draped over the rafters like a slab of beef hung up in a smokehouse.

She opened her mouth to scream, but before she could utter a sound, Jason's hand came out from underneath the hammock and clamped down across her forehead. He held her head down while his other hand drove a carving knife up between the rope strands of the hammock and into the back of her neck. The long, sharp blade ripped through her trachea and vocal cords as she croaked horribly, choking on the blood that flooded her severed throat. The steel blade went completely through her neck and, in the last agonizing seconds of her life, Debbie saw the reddened tip of the carving knife rising up out of the hollow of her throat like some grotesque growth erupting from her body. Through a haze of red fire, she saw Andy's body up above her in the rafters, one arm dangling down, as if he were trying to reach out to her, and then all feeling went away as she slipped into oblivion.

Chuck staggered back into the kitchen and started pawing through the pots and pans with a tremendous clatter. He giggled as he thought to himself, Man, am I wrecked! He selected a huge pot and poured a generous amount of corn oil into it, straight from the bottle, without bothering to measure. Then he turned the flame up all the way and tossed a couple of test kernels into the pot, just as the instructions on the jar said. Then he decided, the hell with it, and dumped a whole handful of popcorn kernels into the pot. He stared at it thoughtfully for a moment, then dumped in another handful just for good measure. Then he upended the jar over the pot and dumped it all in.

He rummaged through the shelves, knocking over spice tins and containers of dried herbs, looking for some salt. He found something labeled "sea salt" and figured that was close enough. He shook a mess of it out into the pot, and for variety's sake, he added some pepper and some MSG. He shook the pot and after a few minutes, the popcorn started to pop. When he lifted the lid to check, popcorn exploded up into the air like sparks. He leaned in with his mouth open, trying to catch them on the fly.

Chili came rushing into the kitchen. "Did I

hear you screaming?" she said, looking at him anxiously.

He grinned at her, his mouth crammed full of popcorn. The MSG actually helped the flavor. "It's probably Debbie having an orgasm," he said with his mouth full, replacing the lid on the pot. He frowned. "How come you don't scream when we have sex?"

"Give me something to scream about," she said wryly.

All the lights went out.

Chili screamed.

"What's the matter?" Chuck said, frightened.

"Nothin'. I was just practicing."

"Well, don't *do* that to me!" he said, taking a deep breath to calm himself. The only light in the kitchen was the blue flame from the stove. Chuck quickly removed the pot from the flame before all the popcorn burned. He heard Chili rummaging through the kitchen drawers, and a moment later, she clicked on a flashlight and handed it to him.

"Here," she said, "go down in the cellar and check the fuse box."

"In the dark?" he said. *"Alone?"*

Ever since childhood, he'd had an irrational fear of the dark that, unlike other children, he had never managed to outgrow. When he slept alone, he still slept with a nightlight. In the darkness, coats hanging in open closets took on the ominous aspect of strangers lurking in the shadows, waiting to leap out and attack him. A bathrobe hanging on a hook screwed into the back of a door looked like some sinister ogre reaching out for him. Furniture took on soft, indefinite shapes in the darkness, which his imagination transformed into ravening monsters crouching and ready to spring. He knew, of course, that there were no strangers hiding in the closet, only coats, and that there was no ogre standing by the door, but just his bathrobe on a hanger, and that it wasn't a werewolf crouching in the corner, but merely an armchair. Intellectually, he knew that, but emotionally, he was convinced that strange, malevolent beings crept out of the woodwork when the lights were out.

"Be a man, man," Chili said, taking a lantern down from a windowsill and setting it on the table to prime and light it. Chuck sighed with resignation and headed for the basement stairs.

He opened the door and shined the light down the steep steps. He wrinkled his nose as he smelled the damp, musty odor coming up from the basement. Slowly, he tiptoed down the steps, talking to himself as he went.

"There's nothin' to be afraid of, man," he said, moistening his lips as he carefully picked his way down the stairs. "So what if it's dark? Nothin' to be afraid of."

He got down to the bottom of the stairs and his bare feet stepped into water puddled on the cellar floor. Great, he thought, the damn cellar's flooded. The water came up to his ankles. He swallowed hard and tried not to think about all the things that could be swimming around in that dirty water—rats, snakes, leeches—*leeches*? In a cellar? Come on, man, he thought, get it together. Don't go freakin' out just 'cause there's a little water on the floor!

He swung the flashlight beam around and it fell on a lean, vicious-looking creature with a long snout and glittering eyes. Its teeth were bared in a feral snarl.

"*Aah! Jesus!*" he cried, recoiling from the hideous-looking thing, raising his arm to ward off its leap, and then he realized that it was only a stuffed animal. Relieved, he exhaled heavily and approached it. It was a stuffed weasel, which he touched gingerly and grimaced. Who the hell would want to keep such a thing around? Well, apparently no one, because they had stuck it in the basement. He swept the beam around over wooden crates and moldering cardboard boxes, some closed and some open, containing all sorts of junk and bric-a-brac.

The flashlight beam fell on an old 1940's

nudie pinup. He grinned with appreciation. "All right!" As soon as he got the situation with the fuse box straightened out, he'd roll the poster up and take it with him.

There was a noise behind him that sounded like a footfall on the stairs. He quickly spun around.

"Who's there?"

Upstairs, Chili discarded Chuck's popcorn disaster and started fresh with a new pot. It was a good thing Chuck didn't have to cook, she thought. He'd be utterly lost in a world without burger drive-ins, taco joints and pizza parlors. She made a face as she dumped the greasy popcorn and started to shake the second pot. Suddenly, something heavy fell against the kitchen door.

She picked up the lantern. "Chuck? You back already?"

There was no answer.

She hesitated, then reached out and pulled open the door. Shelly fell against the door frame, his eyes bulging, his mouth working as a ghastly, incoherent wheeze came out of him. His throat was slashed from ear to ear and blood was running down his neck onto his shirt. He stretched his hand out to her and blood trickled from his mouth.

"Nice makeup job," said Chili, turning away from him. She wasn't falling for that trick again!

He slumped down to the floor and fell forward on his face, blocking the door.

She turned and looked at him irritably. He was getting to be a real drag. The death of the party, she thought. "Stop foolin' around, man."

As he died, she went back to shaking her popcorn.

Chuck swept the flashlight beam all around the basement, but there didn't seem to be anyone else in the cellar. Yet he was certain he had heard something. Only the house settling, he told himself. Old places like this always creak and groan. He took a deep breath to settle his nerve and exhaled slowly. Damn, he hated being alone in the dark! It was giving him the creeps. If it wasn't for the flashlight, he'd never have been able to handle it. He moved deeper into the cellar, sweeping the flashlight beam back and forth and, finally, it fell on a gray steel fuse box mounted on the far wall. At last, he thought.

He moved closer, peering at the box. It had been left open and he could see that it wasn't exactly up to code. The old fuses had been replaced with circuit breakers, but the wiring was all exposed and the old cloth insulation was badly frayed. Not very safe at all. Man, he thought, this just is not my day.

He shined the flashlight into the box and saw that the main breaker had clicked into the "off" position. It must have been a power surge. Gingerly, he reached out, all too aware of the fact that he was standing barefoot in ankle-deep water, and quickly clicked the breaker switch back to the "on" position. Then he pulled his finger back quickly. The dim forty-watt bulb in the fixture overhead flickered on and Chuck sighed with relief that it was over and he could go back to his munchies. He was beginning to think he'd never get out of that basement.

"That's better," he said, turning to go back upstairs.

He gasped at the sight of the huge, backlit figure standing close behind him. The flashlight beam fell on the white hockey mask, and before Chuck could take another breath, Jason's hand shot out and closed around his throat, seizing him and lifting him straight up off the floor. Chuck wriggled like a fish in the immensely powerful grip, his eyes bulging wildly as he vainly gasped for air.

With one smooth motion, Jason hurled him right into the open fuse box. Electricity crackled as Chuck slammed back into the old wiring and his bare feet hit the water. Splayed out against the fuse box as if he were crucified, Chuck jerked and writhed as the juice coursed through his body and electrocuted him. Sparks shot out of the box, the light bulb overhead flickered madly, and the smell of burning flesh filled the musty cellar.

Chili stood at the stove, frowning up at the lights as they started to blink rapidly on and off. "What's goin' *on*?" she said to herself, wondering what the hell Chuck was doing down there. Chuck, she thought, will you stop playing with the juice?

She picked up the lantern and headed for the door. Shelly's body blocked the way. She sighed, rolling her eyes. Him, too, she thought. Who needs this? It was enough to make her want to scream.

"Get up, Shelly," she said, prodding him with her foot. "Enough is enough!"

He didn't move or respond.

Chili set her teeth and bent down to shove him out of the way, but he was dead weight. Then she noticed how very still he was lying. She reached out to touch him and her hand came away stained with blood. She looked at her fingers in the light of the lantern and realized with a dreadful certainty that this wasn't makeup. It was the real thing.

"Oh, my *God* . . ."

Screaming, she recoiled from him and ran into the living room. The fireplace was blazing from the logs Chuck had added to it earlier. The flames threw garish shadows on the walls. In her panic, she didn't notice that there was an iron fireplace poker stuck between the logs.

"*Andy! Debbie!*" she screamed as she ran up the spiral staircase to the second-floor bedrooms. "*Shelly's dead! He's dead!*"

Jason's hand closed around the handle of the iron poker he had heated in the fire. Its tip was glowing red hot.

Chili started screaming uncontrollably as she beheld the horror in Andy and Debbie's bedroom. Debbie was lying on her back in the net hammock, her eyes bulging, her face twisted into a terrifying grimace, a carving knife sticking up out of her throat as if it had spurted from her neck. Blood was puddled on the floor beneath her. Andy's body was draped over the rafters, his arm hanging down loosely, his eyes glazed, the blood from his grisly wound draining onto the floor as if he were a side of beef in a kosher slaughterhouse.

She fled screaming from the bedroom to the rail, racked with dry heaves. She hung over the rail, gulping for air, desperately trying to stop the tremors that had seized her.

"Oh, my *God . . . Help!*"

The lights continued to flash on and off wildly

as she staggered down the stairs, knowing she had to get out of the house and flee, run for her life, get as far away from there as possible. She stumbled down the stairs, almost falling headlong, ran straight for the door. It was ajar and a strong gust of wind suddenly blew it open, slamming it against the wall. She screamed, thinking someone had thrown it open, and she turned. . . .

With a powerful thrust, the sizzling, red-hot poker was driven straight into her stomach. It penetrated deeply, crisping her skin and sending thin tendrils of smoke curling up from the cauterizing wound. The breath hissed out of her as she felt the shock of the brutal impact and the fiery agony of the glowing iron. She saw the loathsome eyes behind the stark white mask and then her vision blurred. She couldn't even scream. She was beyond screaming. She was beyond pain. And a moment later, she was beyond caring.

EIGHT

Rick played the flashlight beam on the ground before them as they walked down the winding dirt road that ran parallel to the lakeshore. Chris had her arm around his waist. He stopped for a moment as they came to a bend in the road, gently pulled her close, and kissed her. For once, she didn't pull away, but responded hungrily. Then she broke the kiss and smiled at him.

"Great shortcut, Rick," she said sarcastically, knowing perfectly well that it would have been quicker for them to take the hiking trail along the lakeshore. But she didn't really mind. It was a tremendous load off her mind that he understood what she had gone through and she wished now that she'd told him about it before. It had been unfair to him, but things would be better now. She shivered slightly in the cool night air. "Come on," she said, pulling him along, "let's move it."

"Always spoiling my fun," said Rick, grinning at her.

Something crunched behind them.

"What was that noise?" He spun around, shining the light behind them.

"What?" said Chris, alarmed.

"I don't know," Rick replied. "I heard something over there."

"Come on, let's get home," said Chris, her nerves on edge. They weren't too far from where she had been attacked.

The moon was full, and dark clouds scudded across it. The wind was getting quite strong. They walked quickly down the graded dirt road, their footsteps crunching on the gravel. The leaves were rustling fiercely and the trees were starting to bend. Rick and Chris squinted and leaned forward slightly as they walked.

"This wind sure came up," Rick said, squeezing his eyes shut against some windblown dust.

They turned off the main road and trotted quickly down the drive leading to the house. They crossed the wooden bridge over the dry streamed and the house came into view as they rounded a stand of pine trees.

The windows were all open and the curtains were billowing out. The house was dark, except for the faint golden glow from the fireplace that kept the house from looking completely deserted.

"Seems awfully quiet around here," said Chris as they approached the house. "It's hard to believe the wild bunch is already in bed."

"Yeah, well, who knows with those guys?" Rick said. After that had happend to his car, he wasn't exactly thrilled with Chris' friends. He'd have been just as happy if they weren't around anymore.

They climbed up the steps to the porch, Rick lighting the way, and Chris reached for the knob on the front door. She turned it and the door opened a couple of inches, then came to a stop, stuck. She frowned and pushed on it, but it wouldn't budge.

"I can't get this door open," she said, glancing at Rick. "There's something behind it."

"Here, take this," said Rick, handing her the flashlight. "Let me do it."

He grasped the knob and shoved the door, putting his shoulder to it, forcing it open with a scraping sound. He got it open wide enough for them to slip inside.

"Oh, no wonder," he said as soon as they got in. "Somebody put this chair there."

He moved the wooden kitchen chair aside, thinking at first that the others put it there as a prank, but then he frowned as she sniffed the air.

"Something's burning," he said. "Look at the stove."

He tried the light switch as Chris went quickly to the kitchen. He flicked the switch several times, up and down, with no result. Something was definitely wrong here, he thought. He followed Chris into the kitchen.

"Oh, real smart!" she said, holding a charred pot with a towel around the handle. Inside it were the remains of blackened, smoking popcorn. She turned off the burner, dumped the smoking pot into the sink and ran cold water over it. She made a face as a cloud of steam rose up from the charred pot.

"The lights aren't working, either," Rick said.

Chris stared at him, perplexed. "What's going *on* around here?"

"I don't now," said Rick sourly. "You tell me. They're *your* friends." His tone clearly indicated his disapproval. "Listen, I'm going to go on out to the living room and check out what's going on out there."

He half expected to find them crashed out on the couch, stoned to the gills. And if that was the case, despite the fact that they were Chris' friends, he was going to give them hell about it. They might've burned the house down.

He went into the living room, but it was

empty, although the logs in the fireplace were burning brightly. After trying the light switches in the living room, he discovered they didn't work, either. The power must be out throughout the house, he thought. The main fuse was probably blown.

"Andy? Debbie?" he called out, glancing up at the second-floor balcony. "You guys up there? Anybody here?"

He went back into the kitchen. Debbie was scrubbing out the pot with steel wool by the light of a kerosene lamp.

"Everybody else has taken off and left us," he said.

She looked up at him with surprise. "They wouldn't do that."

Maybe not, he thought. And the van was still parked outside. But he couldn't think of any other explanation for this kind of strange behavior. In weather like this, they certainly wouldn't be down by the lake, would they? Perhaps they were outside in the barn. If this was all some sort of prank they were playing, it wasn't very funny.

"Well, I don't know what's going on," said Rick, "but I'm going to go outside and take a look around."

"Rick, wait!" Chris called after him as he went out the door. "I want to come with you!"

She quickly rinsed off the pot and put it on

143

the counter, then ran after him, wiping her hands on her jeans.

Outside, Rick ran down the porch steps and walked around the side of the house, heading toward the barn. He heard the crunch of a heavy footstep on the gravel.

"Andy?" he said. "Is that you?"

He started to turn when he was suddenly seized from behind.

"Rick?" Chris called, coming into the living room. She looked around, but the living room was empty. He must have already gone outside, she thought. She suddenly felt creepy standing all alone in the empty house. She went up to the front door and opened it, hesitating before going out on the front porch. She felt nervous about going outside.

She stepped out onto the front porch and looked around. He was nowhere in sight. "Rick?" she called out nervously.

Rick was only about twenty feet away, but he couldn't answer her. A large, callused hand was clamped over his mouth and nose, holding him so that he couldn't breathe. A powerful arm was wrapped around his chest, pinning his arms to his sides and immobilizing him. His feet were off the ground, and though he kicked and struggled with all his might, he couldn't break loose or even shout to warn Chris. Jason held him as easily as if he were an infant.

Chris stood out on the front porch for a moment, looking out into the darkness, then decided to go back inside. As she closed the door behind her, Jason placed his hands on either side of Rick's head and began to squeeze. Rick gulped for air and started to scream, but the pressure was so great that it felt as if his skull were being crushed in a winepress. A keening, high-pitched groan escaped from his throat, and then his skull began to fracture, cracking like a walnut and sending bone splinters deep into his brain. His eyes popped out of their sockets, his jawbones cracked, and his cheekbones shattered as blood spurted from his mouth and nostrils. Chris opened a window on the side of the house and called out his name, but he was hard pressed to answer.

After closing the window, Chris headed back toward the kitchen, wishing Rick would come back soon so that he could do something about the lights. She started and jerked back as something dripped onto her head from above. She looked up. A steady trickle of water was coming down from overhead.

"Oh-oh," she said. "Where's *that* coming from?"

Frowning, she picked up the lantern and went up the spiral staircase to the second-floor balcony. Maybe they were upstairs all along, but they simply weren't answering, she thought.

Hell, if they were fooling around up in the bathroom and they flooded the damn place . . .

"I don't know what kind of game you guys are playin'," she called out, "but I don't like it!"

There was no response. She reached the top of the stairs and stood still for a moment, listening.

"Debbie? You guys up here?"

She stopped in front of the bathroom door. What the hell were they doing in there in the dark? Her foot stepped into a puddle formed by the water seeping out from underneath the door. Through the door, she could hear the sound of water running.

"Hey, come on, you guys!" she shouted, pushing in the door. "You're wrecking the house!"

The bathtub was overflowing. She reached out and yanked the shower curtain aside. There were some clothes floating in the tub. Angrily, she reached down and turned off the faucet. Damn that Debbie, she thought, what did she do, throw some sweaters in to soak and then forget to turn the water off? Where the hell *were* they?

And then she noticed a dark stain in the water. She held the lantern closer and saw that it was blood seeping out of the clothes, turning the water red. With a sharp intake of breath, she lifted the bloody shirt out of the tub, stared at it with a stunned expression, then dropped it back into the tub and raced down the stairs.

"Rick!" she shouted.

She ran across the living room, opened the front door, and raced down the porch steps toward the barn.

"Rick!" she yelled.

Something had happened, something terrible, she knew it! That shirt had been completely soaked with blood. My God, she thought, what could have happened? They couldn't have gone anywhere, the van is still here, something awful must have . . .

A sharp gust of wind blew through the tree branches and something cracked above her. She screamed as Loco's blood-soaked body dropped down directly in front of her and hung upside down from a splintered branch overhead.

"Rick!" she shrieked, recoiling from the grisly sight and sobbing hysterically as she ran back to the house. She sped up the porch steps and burst into the house, screaming, *"Rick!* Where *are* you?"

The wind outside was building up to hurricane force. A strong gust blew the window open. She shrieked as it slammed against the inside wall, then raced over to the window, forced it shut, and bolted it. Another gust of wind blew open the door and she screamed again, then ran over to the door and slammed it shut, bolting it and barricading it. Her heart was hammering inside her chest, pounding against her rib cage like a wild thing trying to claw its way out. She couldn't stop sobbing.

"RICK!" she screamed, hysterically. *"Help me!"*

The large bay window suddenly exploded inward, shattering in a rain of glass as Rick's corpse came flying through it to fall with a soft, wet sound onto the living room floor.

"RICK!" She threw her hands up to her face and screamed as she knelt down beside him, reaching out for him instinctively, then jerking her hands back. Her hands came away covered with blood and she gave a frenzied scream when she saw what had happened to his face. *"RICK!"*

Heavy footsteps sounded on the porch outside and she looked up, terror-stricken, to see the immense form of Jason Vorhees stepping through the bay window with an ax in his hand.

Terror trip-hammered adrenaline through her system as she scrambled to her feet and bolted for the stairs. She ran up the spiral staircase, hearing his booted feet behind her, crunching the glass on the living-room floor. She looked down and saw him at the base of the stairs, holding the ax and looking out from behind the hockey mask with those demented eyes. He started up after her.

She turned to the heavy bookcase that stood against the wall of the balcony, and with all her strength, she pulled on it. The heavy bookcase tipped over, hitting the balcony railing and sending a rain of books down on her pursuer. Jason raised his hand to ward off the heavy books, but the case came crashing down on top of him.

Chris ran down the hall. She tried the bathroom door, then hesitated, realizing that would probably be the first place he would look. She ran down to the end of the hall, desperately trying to think of a place to hide. The closet!

She bolted inside and pulled the door shut behind her, locking it and bending down to peek out through the keyhole. There was no sign of him. Tears were streaming down her cheeks. Sobbing and hyperventilating, she bit down on her knuckles to try and keep herself from making any noise. He'll check the rooms first, she thought. He'll check the bathroom, then the bedrooms, and when he passes the closet and goes into Shelly's room, I'll have a chance to run back down the hall and get downstairs and out the front door . . .

She leaned forward and looked out through the keyhole once again. The hallway was empty, and everything seemed quiet. Maybe the falling bookcase had killed him, she thought, swallowing hard and trying to make herself think straight, fighting the mindless panic that was welling up inside her. But what if it had only knocked him out? What if she went out there and ran into him as he was on his way up the stairs to get her?

She closed her eyes and bit her lower lip hard enough to draw blood. Then, clenching her hands into fists in an effort to keep herself under control, she squeezed herself back in behind the clothes hanging on the bar. And then she bumped into something ... someone...

She turned and came face-to-face with Debbie's blood-spattered corpse propped up against the closet wall. The carving knife protruded from her throat. She recoiled in terror as the body fell forward onto the floor of the closet and, unable to control herself, she cried out, then immediately slapped her hand over her mouth as she realized what she had done. She quickly bent down and glanced out through the keyhole ... and saw Jason charging down the hallway, his ax raised, heading directly for the closet!

She jerked back only seconds before the ax came crashing through the wooden door, inches away from her. She screamed as the ax was pulled back for another shuddering blow, splintering the door. There was no way out. She was trapped! And then she glanced down at

Debbie's body, at the carving knife stuck through her throat....

She reached down, trembling, and pulled the knife out as the ax crashed through the closet door again, putting a gaping hole in it through which Jason shoved his arm as he groped for the lock. With all her might, Chris drove the knife through the back of his hand.

An ordinary man would have screamed in agony, but Jason merely let out a moan that was muffled by his mask and pulled his hand back. The ax fell to the floor. Pursuing her advantage, Chris lunged out of the closet, flailing at him with the knife, slashing at him furiously. He backed away, slipped on the water in the hall, and went down to one knee. The knife came down, narrowly missing his chest, and became embedded in his thigh. He howled with pain, clutching at his wounded leg. He was still between Chris and the stairway, blocking the hall. She remembered that there was a window in Shelly's bedroom at the other end of the hall.

She turned and ran down the length of the corridor and grasped the doorknob. But the door was stuck. She shoved her shoulder into it, but it wouldn't budge. When she threw herself against the door again, then kicked it as hard as she could, it burst open just as Jason plucked the carving knife out of his leg and hurled it at her. It whistled past her head and stuck in the door frame.

"*No!*" she screamed, and plunged into the bedroom. Without pausing, driven by sheer terror, she picked up a chair and hurled it through the window. It smashed through and fell to the ground below. She kicked out the remaining shards of glass, then squeezed through the window and hung from the sill on the second story. She had no choice, she had to do it. She took a deep breath as she prepared to drop when Jason reached through the broken window and grabbed the collar of her jacket. He started to haul her back in.

"*No! NO!*" she screamed, pounding at him furiously in an effort to get free. But her blows had no effect, and he continued to pull her in. With a ripping sound, the thin cloth of the jacket tore and she plunged to the ground, leaving part of her jacket in Jason's hands.

She had enough presence of mind to allow her legs to collapse beneath her and roll as she hit, dissipating the impact. She was momentarily stunned by the fall, but otherwise uninjured. She scrambled up and saw him throw the remains of her jacket to the ground and duck back into the bedroom.

She knew he'd be coming down after her, and she needed to get around to the front of the house, where the van was parked. She'd never be able to move fast enough. Somehow, she had to slow him down. She shrugged out of the remains of her torn jacket and ran to the porch. Through the window, she could see him coming down the spiral staircase. She grabbed a heavy log off the pile of firewood on the porch and stood against the wall by the front door, the log held high over her head. As he opened the door and came out onto the porch, she stepped in behind him and brought the log down on his head with all her might.

He grunted and crashed through the porch railing, falling and landing facedown on the ground. She stared at him for a second, holding her breath. He didn't move.

She ran down the porch steps and headed for the van. She made it to the door and jumped in just as Jason was starting to pick himself up off the ground.

"Keys! *Keys!*" she shouted as she pawed frantically through her pockets. "Come *on!*"

She found them and rammed them into the ignition switch. The motor started right up and she sobbed with relief, shifted into reverse, and backed the van around.

Jason staggered into her path, limping on his wounded leg.

She set her teeth, shifted into first, and floored it, aiming the van right for him. At the last possible instant, he leaped out of the way, throwing himself to one side as the van hurtled past him. Jubilant, Chris headed for the wooden bridge . . . but the van suddenly lurched, sputtered, and stalled in the center of the bridge over the dried-up streambed.

"No!" Chris shrieked. She turned the ignition key again and pumped the gas pedal, all with no result. The starter motor whined, but the engine simply wouldn't start.

"Come on! Come on!" she shouted.

Her gaze fell on the gas gauge. Empty! But it couldn't be, she thought. It had read at least half full when they pulled in! There was no way she could have known that the bikers had siphoned all the gas out. She hammered at the steering wheel in frustration and then she glanced into the sideview mirror.

Jason was hobbling down the driveway toward the van, limping from the wound in his thigh, but moving quickly nevertheless. Hysteria threatened to overcome her and then she suddenly remembered the reserve tank. She reached under the dashboard and flicked the switch, pumping the gas pedal to prime the carburetor. She glanced terror-stricken in the mirror as Jason came closer and closer. Whimpering with fear, she turned the ignition key again and the engine roared to life!

She yelled triumphantly, and at that moment, the rotted, loose wooden planks beneath her cracked and splintered, buckling under the weight of the van so that the rear wheels dropped through the broken bridge planks up to the axle. Then the entire rear half of the van dropped through as the support beams gave way and Chris's body whipped back against the seat and was then thrown forward, her head striking the steering wheel.

The engine stalled.

Dazed, Chris shook her head just as Jason reached through the open window on the driver's side and grabbed her around the throat. She gasped for breath, unable to cry out as the powerful fingers squeezed relentlessly. Then, in a last desperate attempt to free herself, she reached out for the window handle and cranked the window up, trapping his wrists against the top of the door frame. His hold on her loosened momentarily, and she lunged across the seat, fumbling for the door handle on the passenger side. She yanked on it, got the door open and dropped down into the dried-up streambed.

Above her, Jason rammed his head through the window, shattering the glass and freeing his hands.

Chris tumbled as she landed, then rolled to her feet and ran back along the streambed toward the barn. She couldn't get back up to the road now; he had her cut off. She had to get some kind of weapon. It was her only chance.

She climbed up out of the streambed and hopped over the fence around the barn, looking over her shoulder. Jason was dropping down into the streambed after her, hobbling quickly on his wounded leg, as unstoppable as a juggernaut.

She ran around the front of the barn and struggled to pull the door open against the fiercely blowing wind. She leaned back, putting all her weight into it, got the door open, slipped inside, and grabbed the first thing that came to hand—a long-handled shovel—to drop into the slots as a crossbar. She was just in time. No sooner was the shovel in place than the doors shuddered as Jason hit them outside.

She jumped back with a cry and started looking frantically for something to use as a weapon. The doors cracked and a gap opened between them. In another second, he'd break through! There was no time! All she could think of was escape. She had to get away from him. She ran to the ladder leading up to the loft and rapidly climbed up.

The doors cracked and the ancient hinges groaned as Jason forced them apart still further, reaching through and knocking the shovel out of the slots. He burst inside, looking around inside the dark recesses of the barn. Then he noticed the long, heavy, two-by-four wooden crossbar leaning against the side wall. He closed the doors behind him, picked up the crossbar, and slammed it down into the slots, wedging it in place. Now she was trapped inside. With him.

He stormed into the barn, looking for her everywhere, throwing open the gates to the wooden stalls, tearing the place apart as he searched for her. Above him, Chris clung to a ceiling rafter, praying that he wouldn't notice her up there in the darkness. There had been nowhere else to run. She knew he'd look up in the loft next. The square hayloft window was open, and if she kept extremely still, maybe it wouldn't occur to him to check up in the rafters, and he'd think she jumped. Below her, Jason was throwing things all over the place, trying to find her. Stacks of hay bales that weighed hundreds of pounds came tumbling down as he threw them about effortlessly, seeking her hiding place.

Exhausted, Chris began to lose her grip. She tried to wrap her legs still tighter around the rafter, but she overbalanced and it took all her willpower to keep from crying out as she slipped beneath the rafter, hanging upside down by her arms and legs. As Jason moved around below her, she felt her strength ebbing rapidly and knew that she wouldn't last much longer.

Oh, God, she thought, please, no, *no* . . .

Her legs slipped off the beam. Now she was

only hanging by her hands. Her arms felt as if they were on fire as she desperately tried to hold on, but it was useless. She felt herself losing her grip and she looked down . . . Jason was directly below her.

She fell.

She landed right on top of him and they both crashed to the dirt floor of the barn. She scrambled up immediately, driven by stark terror, and bolted for the door. Behind her, Jason slowly recovered from the shock of the impact and pushed himself up off the ground.

Chris grabbed the wooden crossbar and pushed up on it, but it was firmly wedged inside the iron slots and she couldn't even budge it. She cried out, throwing all her strength against it, but it was useless.

Behind her, Jason rose to his feet and picked up the machete he had used earlier on Andy. There was dried blood on the blade. Chris, still struggling with the crossbar, looked over her shoulder and screamed as he raised the machete and lunged at her. She leaped out of the way just in time as the blade whistled through the air and embedded itself deeply in the barn door.

She raced to the ladder leading up to the loft as he struggled to free the blade of the machete from the door. She was gasping like an asthmatic. She had almost no strength left, and was at the limits of her endurance. Only fear drove her on. She threw herself through the trapdoor in the floor of the loft and slammed it shut, rolling a hay bale over it. Then she looked around madly for anything that she could use to defend herself. A long-handled shovel was lying on top of a stack of hay bales. She grabbed it and hid behind the stack, breathing like a long-distance runner after a marathon as she desperately tried to think of what to do. He'd be up after her any moment.

Jason yanked the machete free from the wooden door and turned to go after her. Several small pieces of straw drifted down from overhead, having fallen between cracks in the floorboards of the loft. He glanced up and headed for the ladder leading up to the hayloft.

Clutching the machete, he quickly climbed up the ladder, intent on cutting her to pieces, determined to catch this victim who kept escaping him and dismember her, chop her into bits until she was a bloody stew so that it would be impossible to recognize that the pieces had ever come from a human being. The killing lust raged through him, blood pounded in his ears until it seemed as if a tribe of cannibals were beating drums inside his head. He reached the top of the ladder and pushed against the trapdoor. It moved about an inch or two then slammed back down. Something heavy was on top of it. In a fury, he shoved against it with all his might. The hay bale holding it down was knocked loose and the trapdoor slammed open, striking against the hayloft floor with a crack that sounded like a rifle shot.

He came up through the floor of the loft and stepped out through the trapdoor, rising to his full height and holding the machete out before him. Just then, Chris stepped in behind him, and with every ounce of remaining strength that she possessed, she brought the iron shovel down upon his head.

There was a dull clanging sound and Jason fell full length upon the floor of the loft. The machete slipped out of his grasp and dropped out of the open hayloft window to the ground below. Chris stood over him with the shovel, ready to bring it down again, but Jason remained motionless upon the floor.

Chris wasted no time. She quickly grabbed the rope hanging from the block and tackle used to haul the hay bales up to the loft and she fashioned a noose with it. Loosening it, she bent down, slipped it over his head, and drew it tight around his neck. Then she crouched down beside him and strained to roll his heavy bulk over to the window. She couldn't move him. He was incredibly heavy.

She put her arms under his side and gritted her teeth, groaning with the effort as she tried to push him out the window. She leaned into him, straining, putting all her weight into it, and she managed to roll him over onto his side.

His fingers twitched.

With an agonized moan, Chris straight-armed his limp form until it rolled over once again and teetered on the edge of the window opening . . .

As his hands clutched at her, she pushed him out the window.

The rope whizzed through the block like a nylon fishing line screaming from a reel when a marlin hits the hook, and Jason fell straight down at the ground until the stopper knot hit the block and the rope suddenly pulled taut around his neck. It jerked his body in midair so that, for a second, it seemed as if he were about to come up again like a yo-yo on a string. But he simply hung there, twisting slightly, dangling only a few feet from the ground, hanged as effectively as if he had been dropped through the trapdoor of a gallows.

Chris stepped over to the window, looking down as Jason's body swung gently from the rope, his arms limp at his sides. She was at the end of her rope as well. Tears streamed from her eyes as she stared down at the awful sight, unable to take her eyes away from it, unable to believe what she had been forced to do.

With a sob, she turned away and slowly came back down the ladder, then staggered wearily toward the door.

She couldn't believe that it was over. A dozen times, she was sure she had been about to die. She felt utterly exhausted, drained, and shocked almost to the point of catatonia. She tried to push the wooden crossbar up out of the slots, but it was hopeless. She couldn't budge it.

For a moment, she sagged against the doors, crying quietly. She looked around, trying to think how she would get the doors open, and her gaze fell on a large, rusted iron pulley wheel hanging from a peg in the wall. She took the pulley down, held it in both hands, drew a deep breath, and swung it hard against the underside of the wooden crossbar. Once, twice, three times, she kept pounding at it until, finally, the crossbar moved up slightly as she jarred it loose. She dropped the iron pulley wheel to the ground, and with an effort, lifted the crossbar out of the slots and dropped it to the floor.

She grabbed the door handles and leaned back, pulling the barn doors open. There, Jason's body was suspended directly in front of her about three feet off the ground.

She stepped back, staring at him numbly. The cold wind blew in through the open doors, blowing her hair, making his body sway slightly on the end of the rope—and suddenly his eyes snapped open.

"*No!*" she screamed, recoiling from the impossible sight. "*NO!* You *can't* be alive!"

She retreated back into the barn in stunned disbelief as Jason brought his arm up and grasped the rope just above the noose around his neck. With one arm, he hoisted himself up on the rope, giving it some slack, and with his other hand, he pulled at the noose, loosening it and drawing it up over his head. As he pulled the noose off, his mask slipped and Chris saw his hideously misshapen face, a grotesque vision straight out of her worst nightmares.

"*It's you!*" she cried, shaking her head and backing away from him. "*No! NO! NO!*"

It all came back to her as she recognized him from that horrible night in the woods when he had attacked her and she had blacked out. Her mind had retreated into unconsciousness rather than face the awful reality of what was being done to her, and now as it all came flooding back with terrifying clarity, she broke, giving voice to a frenzied scream that bubbled up from deep within her and shattered the stillness of the night outside, echoing through the darkness.

Jason pulled the mask back over his face and dropped down to the ground. He bent and picked up the machete that had fallen from the loft. As Chris stumbled backward, screaming uncontrollably, he advanced upon her, raising the machete for the killing stroke.

Something hit him from behind.

He staggered forward, thrown off balance as Ali, his face smashed and bleeding, his shaved skull caked with blood, threw his arms around him and tried to pull him to the ground. Jason shook him off and spun around, the machete came down with a whoosh, and Ali's right hand flew off, severed cleanly at the wrist. The biker gave a high-pitched scream as he stared at the blood spouting like a fountain from his stump.

Jason brought the machete down again and chopped the biker to the ground. He stood over him and raised the machete once again, bringing it down with a savage force, again and again. Ali wasn't screaming anymore, but Jason kept chopping away like a crazed butcher cutting meat.

Chris ran over to the tool rack and seized the first weapon she saw—an ax—and as Jason slashed away at the dead biker with demented fury, Chris raised the ax high over her head and moved toward him. Jason gave a final brutal blow to the biker's vivisected corpse and turned back toward her as she gave a wild cry and swung the ax with all her might. The blade thunked through his white plastic mask and became buried in his forehead.

Chris stepped back, shocked at what she'd done, and suddenly Jason's arms shot out for her. With the ax still embedded in his skull, he staggered toward her, arms outstretched, fingers grasping. . . .

"NOOO!" Chris screamed, staggering back, incredulous that he was still alive. *"NO! NO! NO!"*

Feeling the wall behind her back, she shrank against it, screaming hysterically as he staggered closer, his hands reaching out for her. And then he fell forward like a cut-down tree and landed with a thud on the ground right at her feet.

Chris stood, trembling against the wall, staring down at him with terror. She drew several shuddering breaths and prodded his head with the toe of her sneaker, then immediately jerked her foot back.

He didn't move.

She was afraid to trust the evidence of her senses. She shuffled to one side, still pressed back against the wall, and then went around him in a wide circle, staring down at his massive body lying there with the bloody ax embedded in his head. She slowly edged around him and went outside, breathing heavily, her throat raw from screaming. In a daze, she walked down the path leading to the lake.

The wind had died down and Crystal Lake

was dark and smooth as glass. The night was cold, but she didn't even feel the chill. Knowing she was on the verge of collapsing, she followed some blind instinct that led her to seek safety out upon the lake, where no one could reach her. At the boat dock, she sank down to her knees and pushed the canoe, which she and her friends had brought, into the water. She climbed into it, huddled on the bottom, then drifted away from the shore into the darkness.

She sprawled in the bottom of the canoe, staring vacantly up at the stars. The gentle, slightly rolling motion of the canoe as it drifted lulled her into a deep and dreamless sleep.

Something heavy struck the side of the canoe and Chris jerked awake, sitting up violently and crying out, *"No!"* And then she realized where she was and looked around. It was morning. The canoe had drifted out to the small island in the middle of the lake and had struck a drifting log.

She sighed with relief, then reached out to push the partially submerged log away from the canoe. She hesitated, staring at the log with sudden fear. She forced herself to touch it, then jerked her hand back. She set her teeth and shoved the log away, then cried out and threw her arms up to protect herself as something swept past her head . . . but it was only a duck landing on the water. Chris squeezed her eyes shut and took a deep breath, trying to calm herself. Her nerves were ragged. She was starting at the slightest sound, the faintest shadow, the slightest movement. She counted to ten and opened her eyes, looking back toward the house.

And she saw Jason's face staring out at her malevolently from one of the windows.

She screamed and grabbed the paddle out of the bottom of the boat as she saw him come running out of the house, his horribly scarred face a mass of raw, dark red and purple tissue. She paddled madly as he ran down to the shore and suddenly the canoe struck something with a jarring impact and she lost the paddle. She had run into a large tree branch submerged beneath the water and the boat was stuck. Panic-stricken, she tried to shove the canoe off, but she couldn't do it and she quickly glanced back toward the shore . . .

There was no sign of Jason.

Terrified, she looked all around her wildly. *Where?* Where *was* he?

Something erupted out of the water just behind her and she turned in time to see a horrifying apparition rising from the bottom of the lake, a woman covered with mud and slime, a *dead* woman, her body rotted and crawling with worms and maggots, and impossibly, she was alive and moving, reaching out for her . . .

Chris screamed as the slimy arms wrapped themselves around her and she felt herself being dragged out of the boat, into the water, and down into the dark ooze. . . .

EPILOGUE

Police Chief Fitzsimmons came walking back toward the house from the barn. His face was ashen. In all his years on the police force, he thought he had never seen anything as gruesome as the scene back at Paul Holt's counselor training center when they found all those bodies scattered everywhere, but this was even worse. He blamed himself. It took them far too long to figure out that the killer had doubled back on them, eluding the search party by following the stream down to the lake and heading back toward the summer cabins. And like a wild animal at bay, the insane murderer had gone totally berserk, slaughtering everything in sight. If only they had tumbled to it earlier and moved faster, thought Fitzsimmons, they might have prevented this.

The driveway and the yard in front of the house was crowded with police cars. Officer Normand stood on the porch, looking shaken. He glanced up at Fitzsimmons as he came up the steps, and Fitzsimmons shook his head.

"Looks like she's the only one left alive," he said.

Normand took a deep breath and let it out slowly. "What was that about a *lady in the lake*?" he said, still trying to make some sense out of the poor girl's incoherent statement.

"She must have flipped out," Fitzsimmons said. "She's been through hell. All her friends . . ." He stopped as Chris was brought out from the house. "Here, I'll take her," he said, gently putting his arms on the girl's shoulders and slowly walking her down the porch steps.

She was in a daze, completely disoriented, staring all around her as if she didn't know where she was . . . and she probably didn't, thought Fitzsimmons as he slowly walked her toward his police car. This was going to be a job for the boys in the white coats. He wondered if she would ever be the same again.

Poor kid, he thought. Seeing all her friends butchered like that, then fighting for her very life, using an ax to kill the savage murderer in self-defense. After a shock like that, it was no wonder that her mind had snapped and she started to have hallucinations. She was trembling as he led her to the car, and when he tried to put her in the backseat, she started screaming wildly and trying to break free.

"You're going to be all right," Fitzsimmons said as he forced her gently into the backseat and closed the door, quickly getting into the front seat and motioning Normand to drive off. "You're gonna be fine," he kept telling her, over and over again, trying to calm her down, but it was pointless. She kept screaming at the top of her lungs and trying to tear away the metal grate separating the backseat from the front, bloodying her fingers as she clawed desperately at the wire mesh.

The police car drove slowly across the damaged wooden bridge. The van had been hauled out and towed away, and the splintered planks and cracked support beams groaned as the squad car passed carefully over the gaping holes where the van's rear tires had gone through.

The girl suddenly stopped screaming and trying to tear away the wire grate. She lunged back, turning to gaze wild-eyed through the rear window at the open doors of the barn.

The body of Jason Vorhees was visible through the open doors, lying on the ground just inside the barn with an ax embedded in its head.

"That's right, kid," Fitzsimmons said gently.

"He's dead. You don't have to be afraid. He won't bother you anymore. He won't bother anyone ever again. It's over now. It's over."

But she just kept staring out through the rear window as they drove away. She simply kept on staring and shaking her head.

⓪ **SIGNET** ⓢ **ONYX** (0451)

NIGHTMARES COME TRUE ...

☐ **THE WAYS OF DARKNESS by Joseph Hays,** bestselling author of THE DESPERATE HOURS. The lovers thought they were alone in the forest as they snuggled together in their sleeping bag ... until the two brutal, merciless men begin the horrible acts that plunge the entire town into a nightmare ... a chilling struggle for survival beyond all laws. "Boiling ... high tension!"—*The New York Times* (400194—$3.95)

☐ **FRIDAY THE 13TH PART II a novel by Simon Hawke based on the screenplay by Mark Jackson.** When the screaming rises and the blood flows, it's time to fear again! (153375—$2.95)

☐ **SWITCH by William Bayer.** Two women, two murders. At first the deaths seemed unrelated ... except that someone had decapitated them both and *switched* their heads. Detective Frank Janek must get inside the mind of the lethal genius who had done it ... and become as cold, as creative, as insanely brilliant as his killer prey.... (153561—$3.95)

☐ **AMY GIRL by Bari Wood.** Sweet, irresistible, eight-year-old Amy is an orphan with a terrible secret. Reach out to her and she'll love you with all her heart. Cross her and she'll destroy you ... "Her most compelling novel to date!"—Stephen King. (400690—$4.50)

☐ **CROW'S PARLIAMENT by Jack Curtis.** International free-lance manhunter Simon Guerney is after the kidnappers of an Italian mega-millionaire's son. But when he lands in London with a beautiful woman he can't quite trust, kidnapping starts to look like kid's stuff next to the quicksand of covert deceit, and sexual seduction that lay beneath. "Engaging, skillful, satisfying"—*Washington Post* (400720—$4.50)

Prices slightly higher in Canada

Buy them at your local bookstore or use this convenient coupon for ordering.

NEW AMERICAN LIBRARY
P.O. Box 999, Bergenfield, New Jersey 07621

Please send me the books I have checked above. I am enclosing $_____ (please add $1.00 to this order to cover postage and handling). Send check or money order—no cash or C.O.D.'s. Prices and numbers are subject to change without notice.

Name_____

Address_____

City _____ State _____ Zip Code _____
Allow 4-6 weeks for delivery.
This offer is subject to withdrawal without notice.

TERROR ... TO THE LAST DROP

☐ **BREEZE HORROR by Candace Caponegro.** They're not dead yet. They won't be dead—ever. They were going for her beautiful, blonde Sandy and for all the others on the island who had not been touched. They were coming up from the beach where they had grown stronger instead of dying of their hideous wounds ... and nothing could stop them, especially death, for death was behind them.... (400755—$3.50)

☐ **SLOB by Rex Miller.** He thinks of himself as Death. Death likes to drive through strange, darkened suburban streets at night, where there's an endless smorgasbord of humanity for the taking. In a few seconds he will see the innocent people and he will flood the night with a river of blood.... "A novel of shattering terror."—Harlan Ellison

(150058—$3.95)

☐ **MOON by James Herbert.** Somewhere on the spinning, shadowed earth, a full moon was glowing, energizing a lunatic whose rage could not be sated as it struck again and again and again in an unending bloodletting of senseless slaughter and hideous savagery.... "VIVID HORROR ... TAUT, CHILLING, CREDIBLE..."—The New York Times Book Review.

(400569—$4.50)

☐ **IN DARKNESS WAITING by John Shirley.** What looks like an insect, sounds like an insect, stings like an insect—and comes straight from hell? The people of the peaceful town of Jasper, Oregon don't want to believe that there is a bone-chilling primordial evil hiding in the shadows of their worst nightmares—but their disbelief won't make it go away.... (400801—$3.50)

Buy them at your local

bookstore or use coupon

on next page for ordering.

ℱ SIGNET (0451)

TALES FOR A STORMY NIGHT...

- [ ] **MOON by James Herbert.** Somewhere on the spinning, shadowed earth, a full moon was glowing, energizing a lunatic whose rage could not be sated as it struck again and again and again in an unending bloodletting of senseless slaughter and hideous savagery.... "VIVID HORROR ... TAUT, CHILLING, CREDIBLE..."—The New York Times Book Review. (400569—$4.50)

- [ ] **COMA by Robin Cook.** They call it "minor surgery," but Nancy Greenly, Sean Berman, and a dozen others, all admitted to Memorial Hospital for routine procedures, are victims of the same inexplicable, hideous tragedy on the operating table. *They never wake up again.* (132963—$3.95)

- [ ] **CARRIE by Stephen King.** Carrie was not quite aware that she was possessed of a terrifying power. But it was enough to transform a small quiet New England town into a holocaust of destruction beyond the imagination of man. Innocent schoolgirl or vengeful demon, Carrie will make you shudder.... (150716—$3.95)

- [ ] **THE KILLING GIFT by Bari Wood.** Jennifer was beautiful, wealthy, gentle, cultured and brilliant... but there was something strange about her, something you could not escape.... To know Jennifer was to fear her. To love her was even worse. "As good as *The Exorcist*... a gripping sure-fire success."—*Library Journal* (140036—$3.95)

- [ ] **THE DOOR TO DECEMBER by Richard Paige.** Six years before, Laura McCaffrey's three-year-old daughter Melanie had been kidnapped by Laura's estranged husband Dylan. Now they had been found: Melanie a dazed, tormented nine-year-old; Dylan a hideously mangled corpse. And now no one would be safe from the little girl's nightmarish secret—as the floodgates of horror opened and the bloody torrent came pouring through.... (136055—$3.95)

Prices slightly higher in Canada

Buy them at your local bookstore or use this convenient coupon for ordering.
NEW AMERICAN LIBRARY,
P.O. Box 999, Bergenfield, New Jersey 07621

Please send me the books I have checked above. I am enclosing $_____
(please add $1.00 to this order to cover postage and handling). Send check or money order—no cash or C.O.D.'s. Prices and numbers subject to change without notice.

Name _____
Address _____
City _____ State _____ Zip Code _____

Allow 4-6 weeks for delivery.
This offer is subject to withdrawal without notice.

There's an epidemic with 27 million victims. And no visible symptoms.

It's an epidemic of people who can't read.

Believe it or not, 27 million Americans are functionally illiterate, about one adult in five.

The solution to this problem is you... when you join the fight against illiteracy. So call the Coalition for Literacy at toll-free **1-800-228-8813** and volunteer.

Volunteer Against Illiteracy. The only degree you need is a degree of caring.

THIS AD PRODUCED BY MARTIN LITHOGRAPHERS
A MARTIN COMMUNICATIONS COMPANY